Song of the Whale

Sunil MS

Leadstart
INKSTATE

ISBN 978-93-54584-86-2
Copyright © Sunil MS, 2021

First published in India 2021 by Leadstart Inkstate
A brand of One Point Six Technologies Pvt. Ltd.

123, Building J2, Shram Seva Premises,
Wadala Truck Terminal,
Mumbai 400022, Maharashtra, INDIA
Phone: +91 96999 33000
Email: info@leadstartcorp.com
www.leadstartcorp.com

Disclaimer: This is a work of fiction. All the names, characters, businesses, places, events and incidents in this book are either the product of the author's imagination or used in a fictitious manner. Any resemblance to actual persons, living or dead, or actual events is purely coincidental.

Editor: Sita Bhaskar
Cover: Palak Gupta
Layouts: Kshitij Dhawale

For mother

There is a ghost in my room that steals all my dreams. It floats where the shadows are thicker, and quietly, patiently watches me fall asleep every night. At the first whimper of a new-born dream, it leans over my body and, like a child stealing a cookie, removes it from my subconscious. And sometimes, a few crumbs slip through its fingers and remain.

These bits and pieces which I wake up to, are but fragments of memories: the black patch of skin on Ajji's forehead, that turned darker and darker until it consumed her fully; the blind girl on the fourth floor who never sees me; a familiar song stripped clean off of its words; a broken, antique-looking cheap vase; and a piece of wood with my initials carelessly etched on it. That is all. Nothing else remains. I have looked between all the folds and fissures of my brain countless times. The ghost has emptied it all. Even the face of mother.

"Of all the things, how can one forget the face of one's own mother?" Aakash asked me once during our smoke break at the office.

My answer was short and simple – "The ghost stole it." I couldn't lend my voice to that answer then. Sometimes an answer only strengthens the question.

But the last two nights, something new slipped through the ghost's fingers and shone bright – a firefly. Too quick for the ghost, too nimble, too small. On the vast black canvas of sleep, I watched it flutter and float, like the dot of light in the abyss next to my house.

Unlike most things, I remember how it began. It was midnight and cold wind blew from the east. The air was without any scent. I stood in my third-floor balcony, smoking, looking into the abyss next to my house. The sun, during the day, changes it, transforms the abyss into a large, abandoned playground. I have been staring into it for countless nights now, without knowing what I was waiting for. It hadn't occurred to me that the only thing that could materialize and show itself in the darkness was light.

Two nights ago, in that pool of darkness, I saw a tiny dot of light the size of a tennis ball. It shook violently as if it was having a wild fit. The light illuminated the ground below, faintly, momentarily. It travelled from the left to the right of the abyss. Somewhere at the centre of the abyss, it stopped, motionless like a soldier across the border without arms. I strained my eyes to see it clearly. But the dot of light lingered, hovering just above the ground. It resumed its earlier journey–moving, violent, never stopping. It traversed the abyss, and then; it was gone.

I walked to the bed that night, dreading my wakefulness, afraid of the thieving ghost. Lying in bed, I held on to the image of that dot for as long as I could. I carried it beyond my wakefulness. That night, the dream was left untouched, the dream of a floating firefly.

Last night was no different. I found it standing still at the centre of the abyss, as if it was unsure, lost. I leaned forward, over the railing and looked closer. But it remained what it was – a dot of light. As if it had found something, it moved. It turned perpendicular to its earlier path and began to travel away from me. It continued in the same rhythmic, violent fashion. When it had reached the edge of the abyss, it was gone.

Even now, when I am about to meet a pretty girl on our first date, all I can think of is the abyss and the dot of light in it.

I must get to it soon.

If you walk down the wide, pot-hole riddled roads of Indiranagar or HSR Layout or Koramangala, the bar doors swing open every other step, until you are lost in a labyrinth of doors. The young of this deteriorating nation, with their heads lowered, eyes transfixed to their cell phones, are either going in with anticipation or tumbling out like paper cups. The music from the ill-lit, dark spaces behind the doors, with its leathery bass, jumps at you as if it were pulling a prank until it recedes and is gagged behind the doors again. Like a jack-in-the-box.

Inside, there is a cacophony; of beer glasses hitting tables, of knives scratching ceramic plates, of steely footsteps of forks and spoons getting lost under the tables, of clicking sounds of lighter's teeth as they open to breathe fire over murderous cigarettes, of the crackling sounds of waiters' tired spines as they bend over to listen to their orders over the loud music. A cacophony of laughter, of birthday songs, of humming to half-forgotten songs, of unintended jokes, of half-finished sentences, and of the death of solitude. Outside, watching the hazy world go by, they wait and pray in silence to the gods to send in their sober angels to pick them up in their white chariots and take them home. Sobriety in cities is an inconvenience to be avoided at all costs. I am rarely troubled by it.

It's Monday and the bar is not empty. But it's empty enough for me to find a table where I wait for my date. What was her name? I take the phone from my pocket. There's her message on the screen. Jenny is still 15 minutes away. Two cigarettes away. I light the first one. Is it too late to leave?

Maybe, maybe. In this traffic-clogged city of Bangalore, she is traveling an hour to meet me. A drink or two wouldn't hurt now. Would it? Moreover, after an hour or so, she would want to leave anyway, despite this being the first date and all that rot. Rudeness is acceptable in boredom. But I must prepare. I open our Tinder conversation and go over her messages. While I read, I order my second beer.

Jenny Mukherjee, 29 years old. Born in Calcutta and studied in three cities: Pune, Delhi, and Hyderabad. Wasn't she the one who met with an accident early this year and was hospitalized for a week? Not her. Not her. That was Anjali from Kozhikode. I haven't met her yet. But I haven't met Jenny, too. So, Jenny is into IT sales in… Wait. Wipro? Not her. That was Suchitra, the software engineer from Infosys. So many names to get lost in, to escape into. Never mind, I will find a way.

I will find a way to the abyss.

My phone chimes again. I light my second cigarette. Jenny is still 15 minutes away. She is thirty minutes late for our first date. Weekdays are tough, she had said. Weekdays are empty, I had replied. Empty. Emptiness. Doesn't matter, weekdays or weekends. It's all the same. Labels mean nothing. Hours are nameless, lack character, are devoid of shape, like the drifting thoughts of an old man with no memories. Nothing to remember, nothing to forget. Washed out, scrubbed clean. Sparkling white but without the quintessential spark at the edge of your teeth. Just plain white like the walls of an abandoned house, awaiting an occupant. Perhaps, no one will ever come. Perhaps, all the humans are dead, leaving behind the white walls in an endless limbo, wondering about their purpose. Anticipation grows, fear takes over. So do questions. Why should the wall be responsible for carving out one slice of space from the next, if no human can claim it as his or her own? The passing of time is slowed, nothing to mark its progression. Perhaps, in a few years, mould will grow, and the walls will no longer be white… fuck fuck fuck. I meant, on weekdays, the bars will be empty. Empty-ish. She understood that. Let it be. I look around the bar, to keep myself from thinking about a white wall's existential crisis. Or the abyss by my house.

A girl sits at the table next to mine reading a book. An oversize grey pullover flops over her petite body. It has slid carelessly over the curve of her shoulder, revealing the strap of her yellow bra, which rises tightly over her collar bone. I look around, guessing her friend has probably left her to go to the restroom and would be back any minute now. But the book in her hand defies that reasoning. She flips a page. Holds it close to her face, eyes narrowed. Squinting to make out the printed words in this ill-lit room. She's alone, I know. She shuts the book abruptly and reaches for her glass. She takes a sip. Her eyes hover over the table as if she were sitting on a beach and looking at the horizon. Something has changed. The rhythm is disturbed. The sadness that washes over her face, carves her out from the space we occupy. She's now an old, crumbling tomb over which the bartender mixes his drinks and slides them across to his patrons. A tap on my shoulder.

I turn around to find Jenny, smiling, apologizing, with a face unlike the one I have seen of her in pictures. Is it too late?

"Hey, that's alright. Don't apologize," I tell her and give her a gentle hug. "And sorry I started without you."

"Duh! If I were you, I would have finished half of that shelf by now," she says and points to the bar shelf across the room.

I laugh, she laughs. Hoping the girl in the grey pullover did too, I look towards her. She has returned to the book. Perhaps, Jenny's arrival and our loud, innocuous exchange has pulled her back into the bar.

"I am starving," Jenny says. We go over the menu.

With our orders duly placed, we look at each other and exchange curious smiles. This mutual exchange of smiles in silence, however, is a form of communication, the one that keeps the words at bay. Words will come, there is still time. Our smiles stay on until we are both done appraising each other's faces, like an archaeologist running his fingers over an artefact recently unearthed.

A long nose which tapers into a bulbous tip. Curly hair parted slightly off centre. An astonishing jawline that cradles thick, voluptuous lips, which are still curled into a warm smile. She is still assessing. It won't take long.

Now, what does she see? A black face with a big nose. Receding hairline. Black lips from too much smoking. A jawline, although as sharp as hers, hidden by the thick beard. A decently shaped head mounted on a tall, skinny body. Her smile vanishes.

"You took different," she says.

I laugh even before I crack a practiced joke. "I am good with Instagram filters."

She laughs too. "No, come on. Don't be ridiculous. I meant you look way better than in your pictures, seriously. I swear."

"Well, that's a first." I tell her. My eyes move away from her lips and look at the girl in the grey pullover. Our eyes meet. She lowers hers to her book in a hurry.

"If this is how you look at the end of a workday, I wonder how pretty you must look when you are getting started," I tell her, not worrying what other meaning that sentence might hold in it. But frankly, I mean it. She's pretty, nothing held back.

"Does that line work on other women?" she asks, her voice challenging, her black or brown eyes equally so.

I laugh it off. I was never any good with witty comebacks. I am not going to try now. I look down at my beer bottle and I feel the first wave of tiredness rising slowly inside me. Is it too late?

"Do you dance?" she asks, eyeing over my shoulder, swaying to the music, watching the people on the dance floor. I turn around and see them, the kind of people I envy the most.

"I don't. That's like asking a prisoner if he cooks his own food," I tell her.

Her head tilts slightly, eyebrows try to meet each other. Then she laughs, I don't know why.

"Didn't you say that you are on a sabbatical or something? What are you doing these days?" she asks, leaving something on her mental list un-checked. Moving on.

I take a moment to go over the word 'days'. I need to look at them through her eyes and realize that days and nights are two different things. That you stay awake during the day and sleep in the night. That you build your life during the day and rest your tired bones in the night. That you roll the boulder up the hill during the day and sleep in the night, listening to the rumbling sound of the boulder rolling down. And after several years, I finally woke up, on that fateful evening in Namita's bed, to the clinking sound of a faceless man, sculpting the boulder with his hammer and chisel.

I have only just…

"Hello?" I hear Jenny's voice, with a hint of boredom.

"Yes, yeah. I took a break from work." I shake my head to ward off my tiredness. "Been a month or so. Back in October, I think. What am I doing? What else are we all doing these days? Netflix. I have just been watching Netflix all day. Which reminds me, what are you watching?" I ask her. When you are short of words, you can always fill the silence with Netflix.

Her eyes light up, her voice excited. "You won't believe. I am just hooked onto these crime documentaries on Netflix, you know. They are so good."

"Like Ted Bundy stuff?" I ask. It's true. I cannot believe.

"Yeah. Have you watched it?"

"Oh, no. I haven't. I have heard they are great. But, honestly, never pegged you for someone who watches, you know, crime documentaries. They must be pretty gory, I assume." I surprise myself with the tone of my voice. It is almost unsettling because it sounds genuinely curious. Rightly so, because she has a display picture of a puppy on her WhatsApp, loves her picnics in Cubbon park on Sunday mornings, grew up around uncles, aunts, cousins, and family in general, is addicted to Candy Crush or some such game, and says I am just the second guy she has ever met from a dating app. Perhaps, the only outlet for that primal, all-too-human darkness in her is watching crime shows. I don't know. I have always been bad at reading people.

"What do you mean?" she asks. The smile vanishes from her face.

"Oh, no. Don't get me wrong. There is nothing wrong with watching crime shows. You come across as someone who enjoys her sunshine, and it shows on your face." I recalibrate and smile, hoping to rekindle that smile.

It works. Her lips, they curl and part slightly to make way for the tip of the bottle. She takes an ounce or two too much and the beer spills out from the corner of her mouth. Her hand rushes to grab a tissue and she wipes her chin and her lips gently with it. Her lipstick is ruined.

"Excuse me, I will be back," she says, grabs her handbag and heads to the restroom.

Without sparing a second, my eyes turn towards the girl in the grey pullover. Her eyes are far off, seeing things they don't want to. Perhaps at the dead skin of a promise that has slithered out of it, at the back of a train that's receding into the distance, at the mould growing on a wall that was once white. My hands move, slide the bottle across the table and pull it back. I don't know why. It's too late anyway. Jenny is back and her lips shine.

"Is everything alright? You seem to be in some deep thought," she says, taking her seat.

"Oh, really? No. I am good. I was just worried about your lipstick," I say, with a well-timed smile to my rescue.

"God, it's hard to put a finger on what it is about you that is intriguing. You seem like the kinda guy who takes himself too seriously. But then again, you say these things. Also, just so you know, I don't like serious guys. Good vibes only," she says.

I smile back and sip my beer. Silence and the distance between us begin to grow. My fingers begin to peel the beer label as I turn inward and search for something funny to say. Maybe a funny incident? Something I could borrow from someone else's conversation? Something I had read or watched? I don't remember any. Even if there were any memories, I do not know where they rest. It is as if I am living each moment and forgetting it the next. If you don't remember the life you lived, what do you turn to in your loneliness? How do you communicate this… this nothingness? I hear time ticking in the private silence that dwells on the table. I begin to sink in it.

Tired. Too tired. I am drowning. Hands still flailing above the water. Not too violently. I don't want anyone to see them. It's just my body, not used to drowning. I wait for it to acknowledge, understand, and give up. I try to break its conditioning, day after day. It needs to know. Someday, I will just walk into the ocean, and the water, perhaps a bit too salty for my taste, will flow inside me and fill the hole inside my chest.

"Hey man, are you alright? You look… worried," Jenny's voice resurfaces.

I look around and find the waiter and the couple at the next table looking in our direction. Jenny, her face flushed, is watching them from the corner of her eye.

I light another cigarette. "Oh, I am fine. I don't like serious folks either. They are the worst. Good vibes, yes," I say, without looking at her.

She knows. They always do. Sometimes I am glad for their intuition. The rhythm is disturbed. Suddenly, in this moment, we want to be elsewhere. Anywhere but here. A shimmering, lonely firefly glows inside me, floats like a feather, gravity-less, aimless, lost. She would have seen it too, if only she weren't behind the wall where the music is great, and her friends are joyous. The firefly reminds me of the abyss. I should get to it soon.

Jenny is looking around the room, swaying her head to the beats of David Guetta or someone, I don't know. Occasionally, our eyes meet, we smile and look at each other's bottles, measuring in silence. Words have quietly walked out of us, without the slightest hint of their footsteps. In my half of the silence, I become aware of how simple she is, how unadulterated, how she could have taken me by the hand and guided my steps… 1 2 3 pause… 5 6 7 pause. Suddenly, I call out to the words, who turn around and look at me, bewildered. I summon them, line them up, take a step back and look at my creation. A question – What's your favourite childhood memory, Jenny?

"Should we get the check?" I hear Jenny's voice.

"Yes."

It's too late.

I see her to her chariot outside, wave my final goodbye and walk back inside. The girl in the grey pullover has left too. Reluctant, I take her seat as if I were occupying the front seat in an empty theatre. I order my Jack Daniels and coke. I wait. The show is just about to begin.

The first few images appear. Grey clouds rolling into each other, rendering each other shapeless, not fighting for space, yet eager to fill in every inch. Flourishing with ease, forming intricate patterns that change ceaselessly. And I wait for them to form a face, of that of mother. It's been years, she never appears. Many times, I have wondered, even if her face did appear in this abstraction, would I recognise it? I don't know. The ghost in my room has stolen away all memories of her and wiped her face clean. I have forgotten what she looks like. I am a sinful man.

I wait. And continue to look for her in this abstraction. The grey clouds pour out of the screen and float towards me. I open my mouth and suck them all in. They taste bitter. I feel the clouds flow into the hole in my chest. The dying, sinful man inside me shrieks. He is afraid. He waits for a crack in the clouds for the light to seep in. Foolishness. He never learns. I have work to do. I have some way to go before I reach the ocean, before I trick the dying man into believing that we are just walking to our bed for a good night's sleep.

I stand here tonight and wait for the dot of light, my mind on the girl in the grey pullover. The image of the girl excites a memory inside me, a memory that is drawing its final breath, one of the only few I am left with. In what seems like a long time ago, when I was still in college, the business administration classes were held on the ground floor of the building and the engineering classes on the floors above. There was a girl, I remember, who always carried a red bag slung on her right shoulder. When she wasn't in class, she stood on the third floor with her hands resting on the railing. She was the only constant, like a boulder in the middle of a stream. For more than a year, I watched her watching people. We never exchanged a word, not even a smile. I would stand by a pillar below and gaze up at her. Time has long wiped away the traces of her face that was once etched on my mind. Now she's merely a ghost, still standing on the third floor and peering down. It was as if she had the power to slow down time, to bring it to a halt. Sometimes, I found myself getting sucked into that vortex of silence and stillness. Now, as I stand here in the balcony, I occupy her space, looking down into the abyss. I wonder if she ever watched me watching her. Sometimes, I have this feeling that she was, in fact, blind. I was, perhaps, a black dot in her darkness.

And, as if on cue, there it is – the dot of light. Lost in the haze of a memory, I have failed to see its advent. It has already reached the centre of the abyss and is waiting. It lingers there, undecided, flickering in confusion. Now, it begins to move. This time, it is floating towards me.

The dot of light is drawing nearer, growing bigger and bigger in that frozen lake of darkness. It doesn't ascend nor does it waver from its path. I wait, undecided, unknowing of its purpose. I am told a firefly glows when there is true love around.

More than memories, my mind stores insignificant details. I never know why. For instance, I know that in its lifetime, which is typically about a year, a firefly can only fly for a couple of months. That's when they glow, set their bellies on fire so to speak, to make themselves visible to others like it, to be not lonely anymore. So, it doesn't matter if the love that is around is true or just a cheap imitation. A firefly glows for life is short and love is ephemeral.

I never could understand the complexity of love, the fleeting nature of it. Although I have tried to study it, as if it were a fish swimming in a bowl. Aakash was that fish. He was, perhaps, the only friend I never realized I had until he disappeared a few weeks ago.

Shruti and Aakash joined the office about a year ago. At the beginning, they were bound together only by necessity. But that soon changed. As Aakash, a few years older than Shruti, began to train her, the lessons weren't only limited to social media marketing. Sometimes, you would find them sitting in the cafeteria talking about the people, about the world and its functioning in general. Aakash would narrate to her even the silliest details from his day or from his past. He had stories in abundance. They also came with his signature child-like humour. Shruti's sound of laughter in office was a sign of who she was speaking with. From my corner of the office and from the common smoking area, I watched them now and then. Going by how she never batted her eyes when Aakash spoke about one of his insignificant adventures, it seemed as if she wanted to climb into his life and live it.

But there was something else. There was an invisible line which seemed to hold Shruti back, one she didn't want to cross. It was one of those human things, incomprehensible and foolish. They weren't just colleagues. They weren't just friends. And, despite all the tender moments they weaved together, it seemed it was only Aakash who was forever falling to reach the pit of her heart.

Aakash laughed at almost anything, to a point of absurdity, even in instances when he would receive a new email from a client. His laughter seemed especially deliberate when Shruti was around. It was as if he believed his laughter would make her eventually fall in love with him. So he tried. He laughed. But if you looked closely, it was also as if he was perpetually waiting for the laughter to end. It must be exhausting to pretend to be happy all the time.

For someone who shared those contemplative moments of smoking with him for many months, I made an effort to help him see the truth that glittered like a diamond - Shruti was in love with someone else. At times, I would hold the diamond against the sun and show him its solid shape, its fine edges, the rays of sun that danced inside it. He would look at it, look at me and give a wry smile, the one that sent waves of sadness all over his face.

"Why? Why suffer when you know?" I asked him more out of curiosity than of concern. I thought I would learn a thing or two about love.

"I was in love first. Then came the suffering. In my case, to not suffer means to not love. And I don't know how not to love," he said.

"If it's loving you can't help, how does it matter what's the object of your affection?"

He had chuckled. I wasn't sure why. Was he afraid there

was some truth in what I had said? Was I just naïve and he was laughing at my ignorance?

"You know, it's not love if it is replaceable," he said and turned the idea of love as something absolute. A purist.

I had nothing to say to that. I searched inside me. I had nothing. I had responded with a meek, thin smile, an acknowledgment of ignorance on my part. And in that moment of silence, we stared at our cigarette smoke, that fell into tiny spirals, mixing, diffusing, disappearing. I guess Aakash knew a lot more about the matters of love and suffering than I ever did. In that moment, I wanted to be him. Just to know how it felt like. Not just the suffering but love too.

"What are you going to do now?" I asked.

The sad smile on his face swayed like a tree in a storm. The storm had lasted for far too long. It seemed the tree was about to break. But it was hard to miss what was lurking behind his eyes. It seemed he had already arrived at an answer to my question. A week later he was gone.

The dot of light now lingers at the edge of the abyss, where the bright yellow light from the streetlamp threatens its visibility. I wait for it to take flight, up into the night sky where the darkness still floats like smoke in an airless room. Where it can still retain its shape, its being. But it doesn't. It remains still and frozen to the ground, as if it is scared. Then, in a flash of a second, it moves an inch backward and takes flight, across the edges of the abyss. What appears under the bright yellow streetlight shoots a chill up my spine. It is a man with a torch in his hand. His head turns to his right and then to the left. After a moment, the man turns right into the street. And I, in this moment of fear and intrigue, grab my pack of cigarettes, lock the door of my flat, and hurry down the stairs of my apartment. The sole of my sandals hitting against the feet and the floor, send a rattling sound in the hollow silence of the building.

Out on the street in the dead of the night. The hole in my chest trembles, churning out fear. Exhilaration. Horror. Movement. My mind runs too. Who is he? What is he searching for in the abyss in the middle of the night? What will he discover? I look around. I see him down the street, with that torch still in his hand, stopping, turning left, into a new street, disappearing behind the walls of the house in the corner. My legs tremble, find strength, and they take me towards him. I turn around the bend and freeze. Blinding light. The light from the man's torch floods my eyes with the whiteness of a wall.

"What? What are you doing here?" The voice sounds familiar.

"I am just… could you get that light out of my eyes?"

The man does. I close my eyes and wait for the milky light to diffuse behind them, for my vision to become clear again. When it does, I find a familiar face staring back at me in horror.

"Aakash?"

"What are you doing here?" he repeats.

"What the hell do you mean? I live…" He grabs hold of me, the strength of his grip crushing my arms.

"Do you hear it too?" His eyes are lit up like two dots of light in the abyss.

"Hear what?"

He loosens his grip, his head droops, his shoulders slope, his spine curves, and his body deflates with the sound of a long sigh. He releases his hold on me and takes a few steps back, turning his face away, to hide that mysterious hope I saw in his eyes a moment ago. I wait and watch as his body stiffens, his head turns, to the left, to the right, up at the sky, to the right again. As if the silence was shifting all around us. A moment later, his body begins to melt.

"Do you have smokes on you?" he asks.

"Not here, I don't," I lie. "But I have some in my apartment."

When he faces me, I see that I am right; he is defeated by the thing he is seeking, the thing has evaded him yet again. Silence leads the way to my apartment, and we follow in step.

We stand in my balcony, staring at the abyss that has spit him out tonight. The smoke that we exhale, lingers momentarily in the still December night. Shruti's face flashes before my eyes, Aakash's laughter echoes in my skull, recedes and dies. I have so many questions, and my tongue is impatient. It's one of those rare moments in life when something happens, and you need words to corroborate its existence.

"I have been watching you from here for three nights now, you know. Of course, I didn't know it was you. I just thought…" I stop and turn to him.

He is mute, smoking. We have shared these quiet moments before, countless times. But they were always inconsequential. I can almost hear his heart racing. Our hearts never hammered in our chests when we discussed the newest shows or the newest brewery in town. We would smoke for seven minutes and return to our desks. Life was simple.

"Quite a view," he says, and I hear a chuckle, short, deliberate.

"What is… what are you looking for in the dead of night?"

"It's… nothing," he says, evading my question.

'It can't be nothing, Aakash. You have been gone for weeks

now. Your parents had flown down to Bangalore, to the office, worried sick…"

"I have informed them."

"About what? What is going on?"

He leans back and looks at me. "You seem worried. It is very unlike you." His words sound as if they slip through a smile.

"What do you mean?" I take offence and surprise myself the following second.

"What do I mean? You know what I mean. You are this… this… thing. Opaque, indifferent. Shruti always said your chest is empty except for bones and lungs, decaying lungs from…" He holds his cigarette to my face.

It's true. I do know what he means. We always know what someone means, especially when you know who you are and what you are. I have known myself for a long time now. Revelations are just revisions.

I light another cigarette. I try to remember the last revelation I had. When was it that I realized that I was a man without a heart? Was I astonished at the dawn of this new information? Was I too sick to be puzzled by it?

It was on the day I carried my tea and cigarette to the pavement outside my office. There was a food deliveryman: middle-aged, and his thick, wide, dark face failed to hide the prominence of his moustache. It was white and looked like a still cloud in the night sky. He wore a purple cap and a purple shirt, with a caption in big yellow letters that read – *Excuse me, hungry bellies are waiting.* In one hand, he held a tray with four large paper cups. With the other, he held a phone to his ear. He was trying to figure out the delivery address. He disconnected the call and turned around. He crashed into a woman who was also busy speaking on the phone.

The tray slipped from his hands and fell to the ground. The paper cups crumpled, the lids flew off and coloured liquids spilled out and decorated the pavement. The deliveryman looked at the woman apologetically who checked her own clothes and walked away muttering something under her breath. The deliveryman kneeled to the ground and picked the glasses in a hurry. He looked inside each one of them. There was nothing to salvage. He removed his cap and scratched his half-bald head. He sat back on his haunches; his face twisted into shapes of despair. I continued to watch him, sipping tea, smoking my cigarette. He stood up and looked around. He stared at his phone for a minute and put it back in his pocket. He kneeled to the ground again and looked into the glasses. I lit another cigarette.

I still carry with me a dream that escaped the grasp of this ghost. It is still lucid. It was about the deliveryman with the bright white moustache. He was sitting at the same corner, on the pavement, with his legs folded and tucked under his thighs. He looked calm, almost peaceful. There were four large paper cups in front of him on the ground. There was no one else around, just me with a cigarette in my hand. I saw him open the lids on the four cups full of coloured liquids. With practiced motion and precision, he emptied a bottle full of rat poison into each one of them. He raised the first glass, held it to me.

"To love," he said and drank it.

He raised the second glass. "To suffering," he said and drank it.

He raised the third glass. "To fireflies," he said and drank it.

He raised the fourth glass. "To forgotten memories," he said and emptied it.

He belched before he collapsed to the ground. His moustache was no longer white.

"You would think I am mad." Aakash's voice seeps into the memory of my dream.

He is staring off into the distance, at a world beyond this one. "We are all mad here. It's all relative," I tell him.

"I… I…" he gathers courage, trusts in mine, and says, "I hear a song. It's foolishness, I know. But, you know, I have been a fool all my life. Looking for love where there was none. Laughing when there wasn't anything to laugh about. And now, I hear a song when, perhaps, there isn't any."

"What song?"

"Of a whale," he says. "Do you know why whales sing? How it sounds?"

"I do," I lie. Frankly, I don't remember.

"I hear it, here in this city. Every single night it starts when I lie in bed. I begin to drown in its depth, float in it. Its music guides me out of my room and into this city. And when I am wandering in the darkness, in these empty streets, it keeps calling out to me as if it's terribly, terribly alone and it needs a friend."

"Do you hear it now?" I ask and open my ears to the night. Nothing.

"No. It stopped when I heard your footsteps back there."

I pass on another cigarette to him. Take a moment to light it as it dangles between his trembling lips. "How long have been hearing this… this song?"

He takes a moment, takes a drag, exhales. "I… I don't know. I am not exactly sure. It started around the time," he pauses, "you know."

"So, a month ago?"

"Maybe."

We retreat to our private spaces, thinking our private thoughts. Acceptance heals, they say. It took a long time for Aakash to accept the inevitability of his loss. To finally give up the battle he had been waging against the wall with his bare fists. He had turned to something else, something… absurd.

"Look, Aakash, I can't say I understand it. I don't. But you gotta stop this…"

"Madness?" he says. "You said, madness is relative. I guess you aren't there yet. But wait, how can that be? You said you don't remember your own mother or anything from your own childhood. How can that be? Isn't that madness in itself?" He flicks the cigarette into the night. "You know what they say that emotions are built on a bed of memories. I can't expect you to understand." He leaves the balcony.

"Wait, I don't mean… Look, it's imp… okay, you know it can't be true. You just have to…"

"Have to what?" He stops in his steps and turns around.

"Move on."

A strange, unsettling smile settles on his face. "You think this has to do with Shruti, don't you? Well, in that case, I guess, the others are heartbroken too."

"What others?"

"The others, like me, who hear it, who hear the song of the whale."

It can't be true. I astonish myself by finding that feeling of astonishment in me. I am in a desert and it feels like a mirage, unfathomable shapes dancing in the distance. Even if it is just an illusion, it doesn't take away the fact that I am, indeed, seeing one.

"You still don't believe me?" My silence enrages him. "Why

don't you come along with me tomorrow and see them yourself?"

"Them?"

"The Listeners."

Terrace of a stranger's house. There is the taste of Old Monk in my mouth, mixed with the aftertaste of cigarette. Music fills the night air. There is David Gilmour singing about his momentary lapse of reason. Two men sit behind me in darkness and chatter about something. Their voices sound familiar, like the voices of long-gone friends. Their words however are incomprehensible, swimming just under the surface. I stand at the edge of the terrace, looking down at the depth of my fall. Not enough. Not enough.

As Gilmour contemplates about turning away, a strange music pours down from the sky. I look up and see a giant humpback whale swimming in the vast, wide open sky. Its massive body, an aircraft made of flesh, swims, with slow wavy motions, moving lazily forward in the endless, empty sky. Its impassive eyes, between its unhurried blinks, look at me. It doesn't turn. It doesn't stop. It keeps swimming and swimming and swimming. The slow wail of the music rises. I take a step forward and feel the emptiness below my feet.

My body, jolted out of its eternal inertia, is suddenly awake.

Everything in this world is relative – pain, sadness, madness, joy, love, hate, darkness. I can't place myself in relation to where Aakash stands. He is a man who feels everything acutely. I, on other hand, have a hole in my chest. But this hole, I realized, isn't quite dead. It occasionally comes alive with a strange, maddening gravity. Everything that I run into or runs into me, gets sucked in it. I hear their screams, even of inanimate objects, as they fall deeper and deeper. I hear their echoes, wailing and wailing for nights at end, receding forever into this bottomless pit, until they turn weak, feeble, and eventually become one with silence. I turn inwards, stand at the edge of it and peer down with no fear or worry. Often times, I have taken a step forward, cautiously, biding my time, with the full knowledge that there is no coming back. But I always turn around.

It's quarter past one. The St. John's Hospital road is eerily quiet in the night. I can hear the cough of a sick man from somewhere inside the compound. The smell of chloroform is weak but still wafts through the air. I am standing in a private pool of silence and occasionally, a car or a bike whizzes past, creating ripples of sound which soon gets smoothened out by the imminent silence again. On this still pool, three short coughs bounce off like a pebble flung across the water.

It's a strange feeling, standing on an abandoned road, listening to a sick man coughing in the quiet of the night, with its immobility that underlines the loneliness, the sickness of this man, twisting and turning on a bed somewhere inside. It's as if I, a voyeur, am eavesdropping on his misery. We are the only two living beings in this world now. I know he is sick and suffering. I know that. He suffers more because he doesn't know I am just around the corner. I, on the other hand, find peace in this loneliness because I know I am not alone. Sometimes I wonder if this is an incurable epidemic, this loneliness that we pass on to others with our constant movement in the city. Stillness could be the cure. This sense of movement is an illusion. None of us are lonely enough to do something about it. Take the pleasure out of loneliness, out of sickness, and no one would moan anymore.

"So, you have come," Aakash's voice skips across the still water.

"Of course. I wanted to see what you meant."

"Good. Let's take a walk. I know someone who is looking for it in Koramangala."

"It?"

"The whale," he says, and starts walking.

I look at his legs, pacing as if under a command. I follow him. I look down at mine, whipped, submitted. I try to catch up with him but no matter how hard I try; he is always two steps ahead of me. I sprint for a moment to cover the distance. Yet, I trail behind a man with a torch in his hand, looking for a whale in a city. Despite the cool night, sweat trickles down my forehead and the nape of my neck. I feel a stitch in my thighs. Toes ache. Out of breath. But he doesn't stop, doesn't wait, doesn't speak. Madness is inconsiderate.

What would I do if I looked up and found a whale floating there in the night sky? Would I break? How fragile is this moment, between now and the next? Now, when I am just a man following a madman, and the next where I am a madman myself? And yet, I hope a whale breaches this reality and I cross over and turn into someone who isn't bothered by questions anymore.

I have been tracing his footsteps, as if in a trance, for so long that I am startled when they stop. I look up and find him frozen as if he had seen a white ghost. The grip of his hand around the torch tightens. His head tilts a little, turns left, looks at the sky and turns to the right. He takes a step forward and two steps back. He turns around and for a brief moment our eyes meet, but he doesn't see me. I am not here. His wide, puzzled eyes turn to the sky again and stay transfixed. When he lowers them, he sees me, and I see him. What I find, not in him but inside me, is a man who is afraid, terribly afraid. The black pit in my chest rumbles. Something has come undone.

I take an unsteady step forward. He runs away towards what he is seeking, towards whatever is seeking him. His desperate legs carry him further and further away, into the night, and I watch, helpless, as he turns into a dot in the distant darkness. I look around and find myself at a traffic junction, abandoned, utterly lonely.

It seems as if I have walked into someone else's dream. Everything is alien. The shadows have taken refuge from the streetlamp that showers pale yellow light. A dog, black, indie, a pariah like me, walks past, stops and stares back. It's questioning gaze stays on me for a moment. Then, after whatever it is that it concludes, the dog walks away unbothered. The hand dials on my watch are frozen at 1:30. Frozen. It might as well be true for the world. I don't know what needs to be done. I do what I do best – have a smoke and recall scraps of memories. It's a ritual for I know, soon they too will be gone, leaving behind an absolute void.

Did I love Namita? Did I love her *enough*? Was that love? Or was I, trapped in my abstraction, aping the world? How do you know what you are capable of is true, is *enough*? Isn't there always a better way to do something? Isn't there always someone, somewhere who is doing the same thing better than you? Does that make you less of a man? Isn't there always a better man? It makes sense, of course. She fucked a better man. Wouldn't one always want the best of things?

"Your dick was alright, his was bigger."

But that is not the answer. Not the one she gave anyway. But the one I had conjured in my head. Hidden truth is a lie. Silence is complicit.

I can still hear that voice, throaty with pleasure, in my head. Her moans mutating into names or names mutating into moans. I hear those moans metamorphosize into a word, how it enraged me, how I wanted to hear my name in her quivering voice. Her eyes rolling into her skull, her face flushed, ghost like. The grip of her hand tightening around my waist, guiding me, humiliating me, reproaching me, ridiculing me to be a man.

"Fuck me." Her eyes, angry, seething; her jaw, clenched shut; her nostrils flaring.

"Fuck me, please." The word *please* tumbling out of desperation.

I tried to be man enough for her in that moment. I remember the way her eyes had shot wide open, confused, when I, seething with anger, had thrust inside her, harder. That moan, a scream, still rings occasionally like a shrill doorbell you hear in your sleep. But nothing echoes more than the sound that followed – a name, not mine, disguised, muddled up, carelessly uttered in violent passion. I thrust harder to untangle its syllables. Sha? Th? Va? Ka?

"You are hurting me now."

Sa? Va?

"Hey"

Vi? Kha?

"Hey, stop."

Satvik?

"STOP."

I didn't.

"STOP. STOP. STOP. You are hurting me, you are… Stop… you are raping me."

I left her, carrying with me a name of a stranger. Satvik. A better man.

She had turned me into a sinful man.

Oh, stop the pity party. Just listen to what you are saying. She never turned you into anything. Self-pity is an easy answer. Don't try to wriggle out of this with self-deception. All you did, in that moment, was prove that there was always a better man out there who would have stopped when asked to. You did not. You cannot hide your sin under the veil of love or hate. You cannot *choose* to be the victim. She was. A sin is a sin is a sin. There is no coming back from it. You, someone who is heartless enough to forget his own mother, must cease to exist.

But she *vanished*.

Ahead, a shadow moves. The hole in my chest rumbles and quells all the memory of Namita from that fateful night. The shadow hesitates, its master hiding behind the tree, peeping now and then. But no matter how hard he tries to hide, his disfigured shadow, layered on the compound next to the pavement, gives him away. He can't help but move. He has forgotten the existence of his own shadow.

"Who's there?" I yell, but my voice croaks and fails to pose the words as question.

As if my voice and its hesitation confirm my human form, the shadow steps out from behind the tree. It begins to walk across the street, slow, measured, intentional, towards me. I wait and I see its shape. A man, an asymmetrical man. The pale yellow light finds him in full and reveals a tall man with one arm, smiling, grinning, murderous.

"Hello, there," His voice, thick, soar, degraded, greets me.

"Hello."

"Are you…", He stops in front of me, and with gleaming eyes, completes his question. "Are you one of us?"

The polished shape of his words, the impeccable form of his question, the accent in which it is uttered, feels disconnected from his appearance – unkept, disfigured, ghost-like. Suddenly, his half-torn body assumes a mythical form.

"Us?"

"The Listeners."

"Yes." The word leaves me without consent. Perhaps, this is the man Aakash wanted me to meet.

"Oh, good. Good. Good, good. It's always a pleasure meeting a fellow Listener." He extends his only arm towards me. "Akumal Shastri, the infamous one-armed professor."

"One-armed…," I say. And stop for I am distracted by the nature of his handshake. The dissonance of a right-handed man shaking a left-hand is unsettling.

"The proof is in the pudding." he says and caresses the stump of his right arm.

"I am sorry. I didn't mean to…"

"What for, young man? If we all stopped feeling sorry, the elephant in the room would probably be lot happier," he says, and laughs with no effort to hide his pride.

I stay mute. I am sucked into a world of madmen; I begin to realize. First, a friend. Now, a professor with one arm. I am afraid I will find love circling around this man as well.

"What is it? You seem to be at a loss for words. Is it the thought of my non-existent arm or do you hear it now?"

"It?"

"The song, of course."

"The song. No, I don't. I haven't heard it yet," I say, and correct myself. "I mean, I haven't heard it yet, tonight." I complete the lie.

He takes a long, puzzled look at me, letting the train of silence pass by. "Ah, never mind. You will hear it soon. A Listener always does." He sits next to me on the bottom step, hitching his blue pyjamas up at the waist. He smells like a dry well.

"Is it true? There are more like… us?"

"It's true. But it's hard to find them around this side of the city, you know. There are only a few. Me, of course. Then there is a young man, of… of your age, more or less. And then there is Shantala, who sits at the temple. You know that tiny temple off Sarjapur road? Yes, there she sits every night. Poor, old woman. She thinks it's her Lord Krishna's flute which is singing. Well, can you blame her? She's never heard a whale her whole life, illiterate villager she is. And, well, let me see. No. That's about it. Just the three of us, and now, you. How long has it been for you?"

"About a week, I think."

"Oh, good. Good. Good." He stares into the distance.

"Cigarette?" I ask and take the packet out from my jacket pocket.

"Why not? That is very kind of you," he says, and smiles. The skin on his face falls into a thousand folds.

I light his cigarette and then mine. We take a couple of drags in silence before he breaks it. "Did you know a whale's low frequency sounds can travel for hundreds of miles?"

"I...."

"And that the deeper the whale in water, the farther its song travels?"

"So I have..."

"And in the 18th century, in Europe, people like us, those who sought whales were called *whalers*."

"I did not know that."

"Yes, son. There is so much to a whale and its song. A fully formed whale song is composed of different parts borrowed from all the songs a whale hears in its lifetime. The first part is, of course, borrowed from its mother, and then others from all the whales it encounters. No two whale songs are exactly alike, you know. And believe me, each of its lung is a size of a car. It can blow half of this city to hell if it ever were to laugh or sneeze. I hope the first person to find the whale doesn't share a joke," He laughs, but his shoulders and chest hardly move as if his laughter is too weak to move him.

"You said you are a professor. Did you study whales?"

"Was. I *was* a professor. Now, I am just an old man."

"Right. And isn't your family worried about you, you know, stepping out in the night like this?"

"The last few nights I am wondering this myself. If I would

have heard the song if my wife was still beside me."

"Divorced?"

"Dead."

I take a drag at my cigarette.

He turns to me unhurriedly, "What? No sympathies for this? A moment ago, you were apologizing for my deceased arm. But nothing for my dead wife?"

"I am sorry," I say, but my voice says that I am not.

"Lying is an art, my friend. Fortunately, or unfortunately, you are not very good at it."

The sound of my own laughter startles me. The next moment, with the full extent of this awareness, it's silenced. The man has a way with words, without a doubt. A well-educated man too, albeit his appearance.

"So, what happened?" I ask without giving the question a look over.

"What do you mean?"

"I mean, there must be a reason why one can hear the song."

He looks up at the sky. I follow his eyes and see that thin slice of emptiness visible between the concrete bodies with unlit windows. I imagine a giant whale, gently swimming by, beating its immense flippers at nothing, still floating, gliding in the air like a feather. The odd thing isn't the image of a whale sailing in the sky but its silence.

"Reason? Let me guess - you think it's crazy. That we, Listeners, including your own self, are just crazy fools. And if it is indeed madness, you believe that there is a reason, an explanation, for this madness?"

"I believe in causality. As to madness, I believe we are all mad. Madness is relative. The only question is how far gone one is."

"Madness in itself isn't a problem. The awareness of it, is," he says.

Much like the blind faith in man's own creation – God. Krishna, Jesus, Allah. To believe they exist, keeping a count of your sins, your actions, measure them, judge them. Do pujaris or priests or those imams ever wake up in the middle of the night and become aware of their madness?

I sense a movement. I emerge out of my thoughts to see the receding back of the man. "But wait," I yell, rising to my feet.

He stops and turns around. "I thought I lost you to your reasonings. But no harm done. I have to get going anyway. May the unluckiest man win. Oh, and one more thing. Don't ever mention to anyone that you spoke with me or even seen me. It won't do you any good. And now, my friend, I will leave you to your musings. One last thing I ask of you. If you ever want to find what you seek, you stay clear of that scoundrel priest." He resumes walking, and without turning, he waves his hand and yells, "Goodbye for now."

Walking down the busy footpath of M.G.Road. The shop fronts glint in the sharp, bright sunlight. The passers-by – the man in a blue suit, the young boy with a white cap, the old woman in a saffron sari, the young girl with the lip ring – they all look at me with strange curiosity, their eyes narrowed, gaze disgusted. I wipe my face with the right hand. The curious gazes don't stop. I am embarrassed. I lower my eyes to my asymmetric shadow. But my eyes keep turning up and sideways, to their faces. I keep walking, looking at people, them looking back at me. I wipe my face again. I feel strangely incomplete. I stop at the Deccan Herald newspaper office and look at myself in their reflective windows. I am gripped with horror.

I retrace my steps, start walking back, searching the footpath. I see a man talking on his cell phone. I tap his shoulders.

"Have you seen my arm?" I ask. He looks at my shoulders and shakes his head. "Some weirdo," he says on the phone.

I leave him and continue searching. I spot a dustbin, open its lid and look inside. Nothing. I look under a parked black car. Nothing. I stop at the makeshift kiosk of a watch seller.

"Have you seen my arm?" I ask him. He shakes his head.

"It looks like this one," I raise my right hand, "but inverted."

I feel someone's hand on my shoulder. I turn around and find Namita. "Satvik? What are you doing here?" she asks.

"I... I... I lost my arm somewhere."

The girl in the grey pullover isn't in the bar. I hoped to find her sitting in the corner, peeling the dry dead skin off of her lips, playing with the rim of a glass of Long Island Iced Tea. But in her place, I find someone else with her face. She is wearing a bright blue dress, which has shiny, silvery flower patterns on it. Her straightened hair flows down her shoulders like silk curtains. Her lips, made prettier and prominent by a shade of pink lipstick, move softly, speaking to the man sitting across from her. When she laughs, her lips make an effort to hide her teeth, as if they are being cautious, careful not to confide her happiness in the man sitting opposite her. I feel cheated.

This evening, everything about this little carved out world is the same. The same old music blaring from the speakers, the same old clattering of knives and forks, the clinking glasses, and miasma of human voices. And I sit here, just like yesterday, looking at the girl in the grey pullover who has, now, metamorphosized. Who was she yesterday? Who is she now? When did she recognize her sadness and then, muster that power to change it? What was I hoping to do once I found her anyway? Walk up to her and say, "Let's pretend," and after a while, the elephant would vanish?

Was I too late?

Someone drags a table across the floor nearby and the grating sound reminds me of the whale song I heard on YouTube this morning. Whale, here in a city. Men and women, the Listeners on the lookout. It is maddening in its possibility. So, I decide to forget about the girl in blue dress and her newfound happiness and look up whale sightings.

'Mysterious remains of a whale found in a park in Oklahoma' - the title of the first article I find says. I open it.

'A city worker made an incredible discovery while cleaning up a public park on the banks of the Arkansas river: he found a 40-foot-long humpback whale laying lifeless, hundreds of miles away from its natural habitat.'

There was another similar incident the previous year in Utah. A farmer had found a dead whale in the middle of his field. 'Those hooligans, those young uns, they are always up to some nasty pranks,' he said to one of the news publications. The media suspected it was an alien ship that had dropped the whale in the field. Even the officials had looked for any UFO sightings around that time. The picture of the whale in the middle of a large field looks unreal. The more I read about the incident, the more I realize it was a hoax published by a satire news website. Disappointed, I look for incidents closer to home.

A 30-feet whale was found dead on the shores of Juhu beach in Mumbai during early 2016. There was another incident in which about 80 short-finned whales were stranded along the 15-km beach stretch of Thoothukudi, a port city in Tamil Nadu. Within a few hours, about 80 whales had beached themselves. The rescue workers tried dragging some of them back to the water. But the more they did, the more the whales swam back to the shore as if they were afraid of the waters, their home. As if they were running away from something. By the end of the day, 45 whales had died on the beach. I wonder what made them choose death over water, while the rest of them returned to the ocean.

A whale song, made of complex patterns of moans, squeaks, whistles, and other such sounds, go on for hours at end. Some believe the song helps whales communicate, a mating call or a threat. I imagine a giant humpback whale, with its lazy eyes, gently swimming in the clear blue waters, singing its deep, mysterious song, full of memories and promises. Another whale hears, its heart beating with anticipation, sings back its presence. And their voices guide them to each other, across vast distances, swimming, and swimming until they meet and share secrets from the depths of the ocean.

"… it keeps calling out to me as if it's terribly, terribly alone and it needs a friend," Aakash's voice, distant, solitary, comes back to me. I look for a waiter, find one, and as he begins to walk towards me, I scribble in the air, the universal gesture for *I'm ready to settle my tab*.

An hour has passed and Aakash hasn't turned up. Perhaps, he went the other way, to a new place of discovery. Maybe, the one-armed professor is out exploring too. At that thought, my legs begin to move.

It's half past one and the night is dead, frozen, like a corpse. And I walk in this enormous grave, where the only rattling sound is that of my own footsteps. The roads are marked with cones of yellow light from the lampposts. I walk towards one, and my shadow slides under my feet. Perhaps, it's true. Shadows are dead skins of our souls.

There is a woman under one of the lampposts. She stands absolutely still. I would have mistaken her for a statue if she hadn't moved her head on hearing my footsteps. Her eyes are covered in the shadow of her brow. But she watches me; her head swivels like a needle following the North pole. I wonder if she is a Listener. I wonder if she's there at all.

A dog, black as the night, joins me. It circles me and jogs ahead as if I were taking it home. With its tongue lolling from the corner of its frothing mouth, sniffing at every object it finds along the way, it walks not knowing I am heading nowhere.

A cab drives by, followed by a man on motorbike. The puttering engine sounds cause ripples in the dreams of people sleeping in their warm beds in the houses on either side of the street. Soft, distant sounds probe at their subconscious where all that is real and unreal blend to create a world of possibility and that of equal improbability. "It is only a dream," a mother whispers, wiping away the tears of her child. The lizard on the wall, wriggles its tail, watching the mother and her child, taking refuge under the certainty of their bed lamp.

As if disapproving of my aimlessness, the dog stops and stares back at me, as if saying, "You can wander as much as you like. But you will never find yourself on the road that leads you back to your past." With that, it joins a fellow wanderer, a spotless white dog with a limp. I walk on if only to prove the damn dog wrong.

The only road that leads back to your past is your memories. I abandoned that road long ago and time has worn away all its markings. I wander, round and round, in the same old space, hoping to catch a sight of that old stone that once marked a year, a moment, an event, or even a tragedy. But my insides are a desert and a black pit at the centre of it where all the memories and promises have vanished.

I take a drag of my cigarette and blow the blue-white smoke to part this darkness. The smoke forms abstract shapes and, in them, I see faces of people I don't recognize. They float in front of my eyes and their lips move without a sound.

Am I too late? I wish I could drown.

There is a man inside me, hiding in plain sight. There has to be. For here I am, just when the thought of drowning flows in my mind, my fingers are wrapped around the fence surrounding the Agara lake.

The lake is quiet. I am not close enough to hear its whispers. The smell of wet grass and moss hangs in the air, like a dome. The yellow, blue and red neon lights from the nearby buildings float on the water surface, shimmering, untouched. The stone pavement that surrounds it, where the men and women jog and walk their dogs in the mornings, is plunged in darkness. I have known silence all my life. But the silence that rests by this lake is peaceful. But how I wish the whale swims in it. But it doesn't. Madness doesn't create matter.

Without warning, my legs tear me away from the fence and resume their journey towards whatever it is they hope to find. They don't stop, even though they are hurting. I can feel the bones in my knees, the muscles in my thighs are on fire. But they walk on. I have nowhere else to go.

All the travellers have gone to their destination. At two in the night, the bus stop is abandoned like the freshly dug grave of a man who decided to live on. I sit and I light my cigarette. Sweat, that was trapped in my flesh for years, runs down my skin. Strangely, my mind, it seems, has been rinsed too. It has rained inside me. All the rusty leaves have been washed clean. I look around and find all the emptiness I have gathered with my bare hands. I struggle against a strange desire, a desire to speak, to reach out to a human being. Suddenly, the hole in my chest comes alive. It grows, expands, turns heavier and heavier with every breath I take until I double over, tired knees arresting my fall. The cigarette from my hand slips, falls to the ground. I see the red dot rolling over and away. It stops. I watch the tip glow in the dark. I breathe. Slow. In and out. In and out. But this is it. I am finally drowning. My arms have stopped flailing…

A shrill cry, a piercing scream.

I touch my cheeks. They are wet not from tears but from sweating. I clamp down on my mouth to stifle any rogue cries escaping me. But I hear the cry again. I look over my shoulder, where the sound comes from. I see a man, across the street, sitting on the ground, his back against the compound. His head hangs between his knees, his angry hands pull at his hair. A human being in grief or just another madman. Curiosity killed the cat. Nothing else matters anyway. I cross the street.

The sound of my footsteps seems to kill whatever he is suffering from. He rises to his feet and stares at me. A thin man. No. A thin young boy. No older than twenty-five or so. His untrimmed, sparse beard fails to hide his bony face, over which his fair skin stretches like duct tape.

"I don't have any money," he says and looks to his left and then to his right.

"I am not here for your money. I hear it too. I am a Listener," I tell him.

His face convulses, twisting into shapes of despair and agony. His ears perk up at my words, his wide eyes roll around in their sockets like marbles, unsure what to look at, and his lips move but no words come out.

"It's alright. You don't have to be afraid," I say.

"Do you… do you hear her?" he asks and looks over his shoulder.

"Her?" I follow his eyes and find the faint light from the lamppost falling on scores and scores of graves behind the compound wall. "Who's in there?"

"Fatima aunty." His eyes return to find me confused. "She was my maid."

"Oh." My confusion doubles. "What happened to her?"

"I killed her."

I look at him for a full minute. In this silence, we measure each other. I take out the cigarette packet from my jacket.

"Cigarette?" I ask him.

Early this year, I moved from Ranchi to Bangalore to start my bachelor's course in journalism at Commits. You know the college? Yes, it's just around that corner. I had never stayed away from home, you know. This was to be my first. I was excited about this new chapter in my life: the thrill of living in a city, of making new friends, of new experiences and all that. But most importantly, it was my dream of… of becoming a writer. I had finally like a place, you know, where I would be left undisturbed, away from the everyday demands of a family. Do this, do that. Come here, go there. This new city and my own place, it was like very freeing at the beginning. In fact, everything did begin as I had hoped. I enrolled in the college, rented a flat for myself, began my studies, aced my tests, like every little thing was perfect.

I had also made like a list of books I would read and list of themes I would write about. Every day, soon after college, I would return home and read and write through the evenings, through the nights. I was in a glorious urgency, to put it lightly.

Then, I fell sick.

My mother flew down to Bangalore at the news. She being worried sick and all. I was suffering from a serious case of food poisoning and she just couldn't keep herself away. She's always been like that. She made such a fuss too when I got a seat here and told her I want to move to Bangalore for studies. Anyway, so. It took a couple of weeks, but mother nursed me back to good health. And just before mother flew back home, she hired a cook for me, you know. "No more outside food for you," she said, and left me in the good care of Fatima.

Fatima was old, like in 40s or something. She was widowed recently, her husband dead from too much drinking. But she didn't come across all sad about it. On the contrary, she was very chatty. She either talked without taking a breath or laughed constantly. She had like an 8-year-old daughter whom she was raising all by herself. She made money by cooking food for bachelors living in her locality. I was her sixth customer, she told me. Despite all the problems of a single mother, she seemed happy. It was apparent when she was around. She had worked hard to get there, I knew.

Her happiness was contagious to an extent that it annoyed a few people. People she met were like blank pages in a diary and she would fill them up with her day's little, insignificant stories. "I woke up late today, bhaiyya," "Milk has become so expensive, bhaiyya," "My daughter is having a bad hair fall. This tanker water is very bad for hair, bhaiyya," and so on, endlessly.

She agreed to cook for me for a meagre Rs. 2000 monthly salary. "Correct hai, bhaiyya," she said, "I heard about your food poisoning. You need to eat good food when you are reading those big books. Healthy. My daughter's books are like this big and she's only in first standard." She laughed and rushed out to buy vegetables for dinner.

"My daughter, no? She is one scaredy cat. She is terrorized even by the sound of pigeons. She calls them purr-purrs. She hates them," she said, while cooking dinner, laughing away.

The next evening, on her second day, Fatima talked about her dream with me, you know. She… she… can I get another cigarette? Thank you.

Fatima wanted to see the majestic, snow covered Himachal with her own eyes once in her life. When she was young, she could never travel. Poverty was a disease passed on from generation to generation in her family. When she got married, she was confined to the kitchen. Now, when she was neither young nor a wife, she could realize her dream. A rare privilege. It was a dream she had hidden away from her impossible poverty. On her second day, she secretly confided in me that she had begun to save money, hiding it from her relatives, even from her own daughter. Three more months of savings and, together with her daughter, she could board that red Himachal Travels bus she saw every day leaving from the bus station next to her house. She was like beaming when she spoke about it.

A week after her joining, Fatima… she… she complained about the pressure ring of the cooker which was worn-out. She couldn't cook rice or dal with it in the cooker. "I will manage with the smaller vessels, bhaiyya. But buy a new pressure ring when you go to the shop next time," she had said. Fuck. Sorry.

She.. she cooked dinner every night using other vessels, but it would take a lot of time, you know. She managed with it for like the first fifteen days or so. But mine being the last house she visited, she would often reach home late to her daughter who would confine herself to the room, afraid of everything around. One day, Fatima tried the cooker with the frayed pressure ring. And, it worked.

"I will manage with the cooker for now, bhaiyya. It works. But please get a new one," she said. I said I would.

But I was always in a hurry, you know. I had stuff to do. Stories to write, books to read. And then there was all this college work pressure. I calculated the amount of time I would spend looking for the pressure ring, waiting in queue to pay for it. And every day I had something or the other on my mind. *I need to finish reading four chapters of the novel today. I need to clock 2000 words today.* And I would forget about Fatima's request. It was least of my priorities. Plus, she was doing just fine with what I had.

Fatima continued to cook using the frayed ring. It worked for four straight days. But… but on the fifth day, the cooker exploded.

Fatima survived the blast. But the shrapnel had found her eyes and her breasts. Damaged her irreparably. She was completely blinded, and her body began to wither faster than the doctors had expected.

I grieved and grieved and grieved. I truly did. It was my doing. I knew that. How could it not be? But my guilt could not undo what happened to Fatima. My parents took care of all her hospital expenditures, you know. I took care of her daughter. I stopped going to college, stopped writing. I spent more and more time in the hospital. I felt my guilt ease up a little.

"Don't harm yourself, bhaiyya. It is not your fault. I should not have used the ring. You couldn't have known this would happen. Not your fault." She tried to rid me of my guilt. It wasn't enough.

I withdrew from the world, only inhabiting that of Fatima and her daughter. They became the centre of my world, of my thoughts. But it wasn't just about what she had lost. There was something else which was bigger than the explosion. It was Fatima's dream. I had inherited it.

Every night, I suffered the same nightmare. In this nightmare, the mountains were covered with blood instead of snow. They were bare, bald, stripped of their forest. And from the mountains, a blind woman descended, walking towards me with her hands outstretched. A little girl encircled the woman, pretending to drive around holding a black pressure ring for a steering wheel. The engine sounds the little girl made would ring in my ears all day.

On the tenth day, after Fatima was discharged from the hospital, I visited her house with a piece of paper in my pocket. I saw her daughter playing at the entrance. I stopped and watched her play hopscotch for a long time. I ruffled her hair and walked in. I found Fatima lying on the bed on the floor, her eyes still covered with bandages. I sat next to her.

"How are you feeling, Fatima?" I asked.

"I am alright, bhaiyya. You shouldn't have taken the trouble. My sister is here. She will make sure I am alright," she said, and smiled.

"That's good. Fatima, I got something for you."

"Kya bhaiyya. You have already spent so much money. I don't know how to repay you."

"Please forget about it. And what I have got has nothing to do with money," I said.

"Achcha? What is it then?" Fatima said.

"I have written something for you," I said, taking a piece of paper from my pocket.

"Bhaiyya, I don't understand English."

"It's in Hindi."

I still remember it clearly, as if I have just woken up from a nightmare that refuses to fade. I had asked her to picture every word I read. She could stop me at any point if she did not understand a particular word or the meaning of it.

There are green mountains with snow peaks, white as angels' wings. You are standing at the bottom, holding Chutki's hand. Chutki wants to run up the mountains and you are unable to hold her back, partly because you are unable contain yourself. You begin to climb the mountain. The air is chilly, getting colder as you go higher. Your laughter echoes in the mountains. You meet shepherds on your way. They sit with you and share their food, while a hundred sheep graze all around you, their bells tinkling as they graze. A mystic sunlight showers the valley, touching everything golden. The shepherds share stories intimate to the valleys and the people there. With the stories, they invite you to be one amongst them. Cold breeze blows washing away all the dust your soul had gathered over the years. You are cleansed of all the pain and suffering. You are home.

When I had no more words to read, I looked up at Fatima. She was silent. There wasn't a shadow of smile on her face. I called out to her, twice.

"Please leave," she said.

A week later, she was dead.

That was two weeks ago. During the first week, I locked myself in my room and wept till my body was empty of tears. Then, one night, while I lay sleepless and hollow in my bed, I heard the wailing noises. I pissed in my pants, that moment. It had to be Fatima's ghost, haunting me for my sins, for the murder I committed. These sounds, these… these wailing noises, continued for some time. Then, everything was silent, until the same hour the following night. They continued night after night, eventually driving me here, to Fatima's grave.

She calls me here every night. I do not know what she wants from me. It would have been easier if she had smothered me in my sleep or or… or just slit my throat, you know. This… this pain is too much to bear. But here I am still. Maybe death is too simple a punishment for what I did. It's all these worms that have grown inside me, eating me, chomping on my innards like termites. I can hear their creaking sounds too.

He falls silent. A strange calmness envelopes him. It isn't the worms, those termites tearing him apart from the inside but the words he just uttered that had accumulated within him, the edges of which were lacerating his flesh. When he finally threw up all these words, he is empty and there was space for silence.

As soon as he is done, the young boy walks away without a question, leaving me with his memories of Fatima, her blindness, and the dead dream within it. He walks away without turning once. It's as if I am that voice he can no longer hear. I do not exist. He doesn't even care that I had said I could hear it too. Maybe there is something else he has discovered. Perhaps, it's something he could write about. After all, he is a writer.

I place a cigarette between my lips and take out the yellow lighter. I press the button with my thumb, and it clicks with a deafening sound. The lighter disappears. It explodes. My thumb is severed. But the pain, I wait for it to travel up my arm and to my brain. But it doesn't. I look at my thumb, still attached to my hand, clean, uncut. The yellow lighter lies on the ground, unbroken.

Clink

The sound, it repeats. I look around. The night is still dead. No shadows move. I get up and look over the compound, at the graves. Someone is breaking through one of them.

Clink

An image of an arm, all bones no flesh, breaking through a grave, pops in my head and sends a streak of lightning down my spine. But it cannot be. A bone hitting the mound of mud doesn't…

Clink

It isn't the grave. The sound is behind me. I turn around and wait. It is human after all. Some construction work somewhere. Perhaps, a thief is trying to break in somewhere. Maybe…

Clink

It is meant for me. I am sure. It is familiar, like my name.

Some sounds in this world have their paths, their destination. But they are free of time. There are sounds, voices, a piece of music, that you heard when you were a child, may reach you in your deathbed. It's like looking at the stars in the night sky. Most of them are long dead. But you see them anyway…

Clink

I follow it, tracking it. My legs listening, clink, walking straight ahead, clink, making turns, clink, deep into unknown streets leading to unknown places, until my eyes see, clink, a figure, clink, covered in darkness, clink, fashioning short, mortal flashes of yellow-white sparks in a cloud of shadow.

I stop short and stare. The clinking continues. I peer deeper into the shadows, an abyss that hovers beyond the cone of the pale-yellow light from the lamppost. I stare longer and harder into the abyss within which the silhouette figure lingers.

"Hello?"

The silhouette freezes. A head tilts and the dark eyes stare back at me. It moves and a man steps into the light – bare chested, herculean, sweating. His hands holding a hammer and a chisel. His face is covered with whitish-brown worms, they slither over each other until they uncover his chin to reveal a grin; naked, evil. And in that naked space, his lips move and say,

"I have only just begun."

At the foot of a snow-covered mountain. Magnificent, flawless. Cold wind blows on my bare chest. The cigarette keeps me warm. Silence whispers, negating itself. The stillness of the mountain like the immobility of the past. And then, the rumbling.

The ground beneath my feet begins to tremble. The pebbles on the ground wobble and move. The leaves on the plants quiver. Birds abandon their nests. The sound, deafening now, rises to the tip of the mountain. And then, the tip of the mountain bursts open and red blood shoots up against the blue sky, flows over the white snow.

Clink…

Where has the ghost gone?

The streets are more alive at night than during the day when they are trampled-on by us mercilessly. In the night, you can almost hear them breathing. It's as if they kick up their feet and lean back by the fire, sipping whiskey, listening to Chet Baker, and nursing their tired, aching bones. My lonely footsteps disturb their meditation, as I walk in search of the other Listeners.

I reach a once familiar crossroad with a paan shop at the corner. Now, it has left its footprint on four concrete blocks that held up the now defunct paan shop. I sit on one of the blocks and light my cigarette. There is a rustling and whirring of a fading film reel in my head, from the days when I frequented this place: working-class men and women heading off to work, drunk boys and girls huddled together talking about work or a new series, a beggar with a green walking stick waiting for the traffic signal to go red...

"But we must find them." I hear a voice, and a moment later, a man hurries past.

"The song of revolution calls out to us," he says, but with a different accent and tone, a different voice.

"Hey," I call out. Startled, he stops and looks around to find me. His face is in shadow.

"Hello," he says, and immediately his voice changes. "Who's this guy? Do you think he is a Listener? Or just a lonely hipster?"

"I don't know. Let's ask." The first voice, almost feminine, appears again. "Good sir, you seem like someone who doesn't belong..."

"I am… I am waiting for the song."

"Good fuck, we are in luck. See? Didn't I tell you?" the thicker voice beams. It sounds as if it is shredded from constant shouting.

"You always know, my good friend," the first voice responds, and even though I can't see his lips, I sense a smile.

"Do you hear the whale?" I ask.

"Whale? My friend, I think we should bail for he thinks it's a whale."

"Don't be thick, my good friend. Hold on." He turns to his left and says, "What's the harm in hearing him out?"

I wait as his head keeps twisting and turning. He mumbles incoherently, arguing, the sound of all his voices angry, pleading, joyful, hopeful, hurt, embarrassed, a whole of array of emotions conveyed swiftly. It is as if Beethoven is having a fit.

"It is, my good sir, not a whale. But a song of revolution." The first voice sounds condescending.

"Oh yes?" voice one asks, and the second voice repeats, "Oh yes, indeed."

"The single most trouble of our times is coming to an end. Together, we will not be lonely anymore. No more suffering. No more fear. The song of revolution unites us," voice one says. The man turns to his left.

And as if it were a cue, the second voice announces, "Together, we will not be lonely anymore."

It feels unreal, the way his voice changes, as if it is cut in half and growing separately. It seems they occupy specific space too since the man keeps turning his head. I wonder which one came first.

"Revolution against what?" I ask.

"Against the loneliness, sir. Against the loneliness," voice one says.

The second voice soon follows. "Come, join us."

"What makes you think I am lonely?"

To which the man laughs, a new sound in the mix. "I was lonely too," voice one continues, "walking around alone in the night just like you, listening to the song of the revolution. It was hopeless. Then, I found this man." He turns to his left and waits.

The second voice sounds startled. "Oh! Now, together, we are not lonely anymore."

I offer him a cigarette.

"I don't smoke," voice one says.

"I do," the second voice interjects.

The man takes the cigarette.

"And what exactly do you intend to do with your so-called revolution?"

"Ah, sir. I can see that you don't trust us. I can hear it in your voice. A sceptic. Tsk tsk tsk. A lonely one too, to make the matters worse. But, believe us, the revolution has begun. Oh, and how it has begun. We will unite all the lonely souls until we are one: a euphoric, utopian society of all the lonely people, humming the glorious song of revolution that beckons us every night."

"And have you met… these lonely souls?"

"Only one, so far," he says and turns again.

"Yes. Yes, we are not lonely anymore." The second voice sounds bored now. The man yawns and as soon as he finishes, the second voice continues. "I always find the sceptics awfully boring. Their contradictions and questions are boring to the bone."

"What do you propose, my good friend?"

"I say, we leave him to his questions. The purists need us."

"The purists need us," the first voice declares, and he begins to walk away at once.

"Hey, listen," I call out.

"Find a voice. Together you will not be lonely anymore," I hear him and strangely, he sounds like the sum of two voices.

I wonder where Aakash is, wandering, searching which part of the city, if I will run into him soon. "It keeps calling out to me as if it's terribly, terribly alone and it needs a friend," his voice fills my head.

Suddenly, I feel an insatiable urge to listen to the voice of water. The image of my fingers grasping the fence of the Agara lake floats before my eyes. There is a strange sensation, a pressure on my ear drums as if the silence has been pressing against them hard. It sets my legs in motion and I am soon a puppet watching its dangling limbs.

By the time I reach the lake, the sensation I had felt a while ago has passed, like hunger satiated. The lake whispers to me. Gentle gurgling, soothing, unwavering. The reflection of lights from the buildings on the other side of the lake paint the water with shimmering yellow-white colours. I had forgotten the earthy smell of grass crushed by my weight. It is cooler, closer to the lake. But I notice something strange, an out of sort, a catch of the breath. I listen.

The wind unfurls the sounds of the night inside me: a cricket chirping, crying of a strange bird, clanking sound of a metal, whistles of a night watchman, ramblings of a drunk man. There is the sound of a hammer on a chisel. And then there is a sound that stops me in my thoughts. It is rhythmic, insistent. My ears carve it out from all the mesh of sounds. The more I listen to its bulbous voice, the louder it gets. I wait for it to stop. A puzzling sense of fear grips me. I get up and look around, afraid that someone is watching me. But whichever direction I turn, how many arbitrary steps I take, when I move, the sound travels with me. It's as if there is a strange creature inside…

"Do you think it's in the lake?" A thin, soft voice sweeps the litter of noises from my head. I scan the shore of the lake until I find a silhouette etched against the shimmering waters. Silhouette of a woman sitting by the shore with her arms embracing her knees. She watches, waiting in silence.

"If there is any place in this city for it to be, it is here. Don't you think?"

"I know it's here," she says. And her head turns towards the lake. "It's waiting."

"Waiting for?" I ask. What is keeping me from reaching her? I look down, but I can't find my legs in the blackness.

The sound of the lake flows back. My eyes are fixed on that silhouette by the shore, afraid it might disappear any minute and prove my insanity. But it doesn't. Its certainty is in its shape, its silence, and its stillness, like a mountain.

"Smoke?" I ask, hoping she would allow me to close the distance that is keeping us apart.

After a long pause, a short, sharp 'yes' comes my way. I grasp it like a drowning man gripping a rope. The ground beneath me slopes down and I slip. My body, intoxicated with inertia, lunges forward. I throw my hands down to arrest my fall and land on my knees. I stagger back up to my feet.

"Are you alright?" she asks, but her voice isn't alarmed. She might as well be wishing me good morning.

"Oh, I am fine," I say, dusting my jeans. "It's just a slip."

"That's how it all begins, with a slip," she says, and this time there is a chord of a memory in it.

I laugh and the awareness of the sound of my own laughter kills it. "I am sorry."

"What for?"

"Oh, I don't know. I just… nothing." I get close enough to hold out a cigarette to her. The thin silhouette of a hand moves towards me and caresses my fingers as it makes its way blindly towards the tip where the cigarette is sticking out. And then it's gone, leaving behind a cigarette shaped hole between my fingers. I strike the lighter but forget its purpose.

In that darkness, in the soft pale light that my cigarette lighter carves out, reveals a face that sends a tremor in that pit inside my chest. A firefly in the night. The thin face leans forward and a pair of eyes darker than the shadow around, watch the tip of the cigarette that dangles between her thin lips. The cigarette catches fire, extinguishes and red flames mark its edges. Her long, slender nose exhales two streaks of smoke that brushes against the fire on my lighter, make it quiver. Her hair is one with the blackness around. A sharp jawline cups her mouth, and on it I see a scar – big, wide, ugly. An old, forgotten feeling fills the hole in my chest to the brim. I feel a wave of sadness gush out, as if an old dam had cracked open.

It's a face I could recognize in a forest of faces.

The flame from the lighter is switched on for a moment longer than I should have. She turns her face away from it. I snap the lighter shut. I look at the beautiful medley of light sailing on the lake, broken by the waves in countless lines, like the scar on her face, multitudes of them, floating on the water like deadwood.

"It's beautiful."

"Do you hear it now?" she asks.

"The water, yes."

"I meant the song."

"Oh, the song. No. I heard it about an hour ago. It brought me here to…" She watches me.

The images of her kitchen, her living room, the colour of her walls, the folds in her bed, the groove in her pillow, strands of her hair in her white comb, and her solemn face in the mirror, flash before me. I have no idea whether these images are true to her. I don't know anything about her. I don't know why the curtains in her bedroom are blue and the walls white. Maybe the images are more questions than answers.

"Do you come here often?"

"Every night since the song."

"And how does it sound?" I ask, curious, agitated, afraid.

"Melancholic," she says, and the word is heavy with memories and promises. "And to you?"

"To me?" I try to remember the description of a humpback whale song in an article I read yesterday. "Well, a series of clicks and clacks, sometimes a single note prolonged for more than five seconds. Like someone's moaning at will, you know, in a low-pitched voice. And there are these moments when a series of very short…"

She cuts me short. "I meant; how does it make you feel?"

"Oh," I say and suddenly find myself at a loss for words. I remember the blue whale song I had listened to on YouTube. How did I feel listening to it? And then my lips move without my will and I hear myself say, "It sounds like the voice of a memory long forgotten, crying for help, crying to be recalled as it gets dragged deeper and deeper into the pit of oblivion."

I search for the meaning of what I just said. I do not know. That pit of oblivion feels a lot like the hole inside my chest, from which I hear voices now and then, voices I don't recognize, crying out things I don't remember. Just like you don't remember the beginning of a dream, I don't recall the time, that moment when this black hole appeared inside me. But years ago, I saw something similar, a black patch of dead skin.

Two men with pickaxes digging a hole deep and wide enough for a body to fit in. When they were done, the occupant was brought wrapped in a white cloth, still as a stone. A hand rested on my shoulder, squeezing me harder and harder with every shovelful of mud that was dropped in the hole by the two men. The white cloth was barely visible now. The last to disappear under the heap of mud was the face. The dust settled in between the deep wrinkles on the face, in that thin groove between shut lips. Just before a heap of mud fell on it, I saw the black stain between the eyebrows, caused by applying vermillion for far too many years. The stain had spread over the years, growing darker and wider until Ajji had discovered a way to stop it. There are some scars which only death can heal.

That black stain had stayed with me for many years. Just like the way it had grown over Ajji's forehead, I remember it growing inside me. With each passing year, with nothing or no one to arrest it, it seemed to have acquired a life of its own, feeding on all that I received in life, growing bigger, deeper, and darker. After a while, feeding it became my only occupation. When I ignored it for several days, the incomprehensible voices of unimaginable things echoing inside it would only get louder as if they were aware of my intention to escape its existence, calling out to me, to be heard. And the abstraction of all their voices, blurred the lines of what I knew, what I felt. Anger (the reason long forgotten) became sadness, sadness turned into something unnamed. And in the depth of my subconsciousness, I tried to name it, to give it a meaning. But how does one understand that which is nameless?

"What is that memory you are losing to this oblivion?" Her voice cuts through my reverie.

I wish I could see the scar again. "My mother. I don't remember her."

"How... I mean, you don't even have a photograph of her? Were you an..."

"An orphan? I don't know. I don't think so. Have you ever felt like there is this place, in your past, where you felt... home? Its shape, colour and smell are now lost to you. But you know it's there, somewhere in your memories, forgotten, and over the years you have wandered too far away and can't find your way back."

Like the man with two voices I met an hour ago, I have found another voice inside me now, which speaks without my bidding.

"Perhaps, the whale will take you there," she says. I sense a smile through which her voice is slipping. I could offer her another cigarette, just to see that smile.

"Have you met the others?" I ask.

"I have but only one. Shantala Ajji. Have you met her?"

"Not yet."

"She sits at the temple."

"Yeah, I heard. That... The professor told me."

"I used to visit her when all this began. We would sit and talk for hours. She mostly spoke about her son and her grandson. It's been a while since I saw her. I worry that I would miss the whale when it finally comes to take me away."

"Does she visit you here?"

"No. She doesn't believe in it, that it's a whale song. And I don't want to break her illusion."

"What illusion?"

"Her Lord. And you, are you also a believer?"

A strange sinking feeling inside me. I wait for it to pass. I say, "I don't believe in a lot of things. I can't describe why I don't believe what I don't believe. But, a God? That's one thing I know I don't believe in. I… I feel God is too easy an answer. Just politics of men."

She doesn't say anything to that. Perhaps, she's relieved to hear it. I wait. Nothing. A thin slice of silence begins to grow between us. I tear it apart.

"The professor I met a few days ago said something strange, a warning about some scoundrel priest. It's the last thing he said to me. It just felt too… Well, I have been trying to locate the professor since that night, to ask him what he meant by it. The professor, as it turns out, is as enigmatic as the priest he speaks of. Do you know anything about it?"

"I know what he meant," she says. "I met that sick bastard once. Another religious bigot. No different from a godman or a saint. Parroting verses, passing judgements. He tried to convince me that it isn't the song of the whale but the Lord, Jesus Christ himself, calling out to those who have wandered off their path. Me, specifically he meant. Absolution in the name of his Lord will wash away my sins, he said. He wanders in the night, he told me. Looking for people like us, to show them the true path."

I wrap my silence around me. I know what she means. I have met my share of holy men who have offered salvation if only I praised their gods. Shoving Bhagvad Gita in my hands and threatening me with Karma or calling me a kafir for not believing in their version of one true God. Trying to clone themselves, their identities in me. But this talk of religion and of other Listeners have muddled the space I share with her. I wait for the words to be swept away. I wait for the wind to bring me her fragrance. I wait for her to ask me for another cigarette. And I wait for the song of the whale for I don't wish to deceive her.

We sit by the lake, holding onto our private thoughts, waiting for the whale to breach the surface and reveal its magnificence. A question haunts me. The Listeners exist. They share a belief. Why am I deprived of the song? I am part of their world now, part of this madness. Why, even after walking amidst them, am I an outsider? And it's only through my lies that I can be part of them. Their world feels truer, more real than the world I live in during the day. The thing that unites them, excludes me. The silence of the whale is louder than the song itself. The silence of her is beginning to trouble me more than that of the whale. I turn to find her gone.

Nothing but darkness stretches out in every possible direction. I want to call out to her but a strange resonance, alien yet familiar, vibrates inside me and waits for me to serve it with a word, a name. The hole in my chest rumbles with all its might. I do not know what to call her. She remains, like that feeling inside me, nameless.

"Why are you naked? It's December, for god's sake. How are you not cold?" The girl takes a sip of her whiskey, smiles, and shakes her head.

I look down at my limp penis while she averts her eyes and looks around the empty bar. It's just the two of us.

"It's just… I forgot to wear my clothes." I cup my hand around my mouth and say it out loud, even though there is absolute silence.

"That happens." She smiles.

I smile back and sip my drink. "Are you waiting for someone?"

"Yeah," she says.

"Who?"

"That goddamn Godot," she says.

The ghost is dead.

The day has passed without marking a moment for a memory. I look over my shoulder and try to find a milestone down the road where I have come from. I find none. It's as though I have been walking through a desert, even the wind has covered my footprints with fresh sand. But wait - it isn't exactly so. Not anymore. I see the land just behind me has changed. The sand is giving way to grass. And when I look inward, at the world that has long been left untended, I find something beside that which is nameless. I am afraid to call it by its name.

Tonight, it's different. The anticipation of meeting a stranger, a Listener, isn't rushing me. I am not wondering about where my legs might take me. I know where I will end up.

But I take a detour to Agara lake, hoping to run into Aakash or the professor or the young boy or even the man with two voices. *Together, we will not be lonely anymore*, his voice rings in my head. Together? I have never met the same Listener again. They exist, even if they are lost in their own private world.

I see the young boy up ahead. He is with someone, a bald man, dressed in white. I walk faster to catch up with them. I call out but before my voice reaches them, they make a left turn at the Wipro signal. They disappear behind the buildings. I take the turn and a hand grabs hold of my shoulder.

"What do you want?" The voice is stronger than the grip.

"I know him. He told me he can hear Him too," the young boy standing next to the bald man says. The hand releases its hold on my shoulder and the bald man steps into the light.

He is taller than me, with a face that is as round as the moon itself. Thick eyebrows curve symmetrically over wide set eyes. The nose, thin, chiseled points down to his mouth and his smile. But his smile is misaligned. The smile is perfect. It is as though his mouth has moved a few inches to his left, carrying the smile with it.

"It is always a pleasure meeting a fellow Listener," the bald man says, and his hand finds my shoulder again. This time it is gentle and caresses the curve of my shoulder.

I look away from him as though, if I continued to stare at his lips long, I would find an eyeball between them, staring back at me. I see the young boy is smiling too, a thing I had thought he was no longer capable of.

"I see you have found an answer." I mask my question.

"Answer?" the young boy asks. The hand on my shoulder slips away.

"Something tells me that you are no longer afraid of ghosts."

"That is because he has found God." The thick voice holds my chin and turns my face towards its master. Something glimmers below his chin. My eyes follow the light. Resting firmly over his white shirt, just above the second button, is a metallic cross.

"You are the priest," I say.

"Oh, that's a label I have been given. But I would like to believe that I am nothing but a servant of God and man alike. How is that possible, you may wonder. For that I ask, what are men of faith but one with God?"

"So, you are one with God now?" I turn to the young boy, who doesn't look as thin as before.

"Yes, I am," the young boy says. "I told you what I was going through. I was lost, alone, afraid, afraid of the ghost of Fatima calling out to me every night. But the priest made me hear the song – song of the Lord. I see that now, I hear it. He has cleansed the song of its horror."

The young boy is delirious, his smile proud. I watch a train of snow-covered mountains pass by. At one of the windows is the face of a woman and a child. Those faces that were abandoned for the song of the Lord.

"And Fatima?"

"She's with the Lord too, you know. She found peace at last. Whatever dream she had, she is living it right now, as we speak," the priest says, and looks up at the sky.

"Did you just say she is *living* right now?"

"Ah, I hear that voice in you, the one I have heard in countless others. The voice of a rationalist."

"Does that make you irrational?"

The priest looks towards the young boy, though his out-of-place smile faces me. "Walk with us," he says, "we have someone to meet, and we don't want to be late. Let's speak while we walk."

We begin to walk. The priest has inserted himself between me and the young boy as if he were guarding him.

"Being rational is good. Being too rational however is foolishness. It makes one blind to the point where rationality itself becomes a vice. And a life full of such vice has no place for the Lord. So, no, it doesn't make us irrational, my son. It makes us…"

"Do not call me that," I command.

"Call you what?" His voice hardly wavers.

"Son."

"Please accept my apologies. I see you are not there yet," he says as though he was, through this walk, taking me somewhere, a place that holds the power to call me 'son.'

"Where are we going?"

"My young friend here spoke of a blind man. We are on our way to meet him."

"And what is this blind man to you?"

"Well, of course, someone who has lost his path, and not just in the darkness of this night, in that which is inside him. You will know what I mean when you meet him," he says.

"I take it that he is a Listener too."

"He is. But this young boy told me that the man is looking for Death. A man searching for his own Death, is there a bigger sin than that? He thinks it's Death calling out to him. He needs our help to make him see the light."

"Ah, I see you are on a rescue mission. And you no longer feel responsible for Fatima's death?" I ask the young boy.

"I never said I wasn't responsible. She's passed into the other world because of me. But her passing away was meant to help me find the Lord. It was part of His plan," the young boy says, surprising me with the conviction in his voice and the borrowed words.

"I don't get it," I say, and truly I don't. "She died because of your ignorance. Now, her child suffers too. How is it fair that all this was designed to make *you* see the light?"

I hear a chink in the priest's voice as he says, "That... that, yes, that is true. She suffered. But who are we to question the Lord's plan? Suffering is nothing more than a path to His kingdom. In grief, we must embrace Him. It is the only antidote to all the miseries in this mortal world."

"You know, I wonder how Fatima feels about all this, knowing that her life and, well, her death too was just a means to an end, serving your purpose. A purpose to show a young boy the path to the Lord. Poor woman."

The priest looks at me and his mouth has receded to where it's supposed to be, still and frozen under his nose. What have we reduced a helpless woman's life to? How can men trade their sins, their grief with salvation? I could grieve the rest of my life, if it meant remembering that which is lost and forgotten. I wouldn't trade memories for anything, not even the Lord.

I keep my eyes on the priest and ask the young boy, "How does the song sound like now? Is it different?"

"You still don't get it, do you?" the young boy says. "Once you realize its meaning, it stops. I don't hear the song anymore. It has guided me to where I need to be."

"Where is that?"

"Right here, by the priest. By the Lord, where there is peace."

All that was needed for the boy was a promise to escape to, abandon his grief, the consequences of his action. I turn to the priest and see that his mouth has shifted its place. Wedged in his left cheek, where it is smiling.

Defeated. I guess I had already lost, only I did not know it. The priest had the young boy under his wings, washed away his grief, emptied him of his memories and filled it with hymns and hallelujahs. I wonder how many more Listeners have already surrendered their memories, their promises to this man. How many of them have abandoned the whale for the Lord? How many more to go? Oddly, I feel violated, a new world I had entered, desecrated. I have to get away from him. Return to a place where I feel… not lonely.

"I will leave you two with your Lord," I say, and walk away from them.

"Wait, my *son*, don't you want your sins absolved?" he says, and the word 'son' stands out, misaligned like his smile.

I accept my defeat and smile in acknowledgement. He knows. He doesn't wait for an answer, any words in return. The question wasn't about me joining them in their quest for the blind man. The question was only a vehicle to carry something I had rejected.

Son.

A moment ago, I was walking. Now without my knowledge, I am running down Sarjapur Road, on my way to the lake. I am in no hurry. Yet I am running. I look down at my legs and command them to stop. They don't. I look around and I see everything trembling - the trees, the lampposts, the parked cars, the garbage trucks, and all the shadows that have enveloped them. I feel my jaw hitting against my upper teeth. I feel the muscles in my thighs shaking, my ribcage fighting hard from collapsing. I can feel the bones in my feet. I feel the sweat beads dropping of my chin, I feel the tips of my ears turning cold against the wind. I feel the warm blood gushing inside them. And I feel something strange crawling up from under the pit in my chest. The screeching sound of its claws scratching against my insides, the grumbling roar, though feeble but present, rises. And I run harder. I am afraid I understand the pit at last. It's home, home for a monster I had long buried and forgotten. I hear him now.

"Where do you think you are running to?" a voice outside me calls out to me.

Across the street I see the bare-chested man standing under a lamppost. His wide, gleaming eyes follow me as I run past him. The skin on his dark face is glistening. He holds out his hand to reveal what they are concealing – a hammer and a chisel.

"I have only just begun, son," he shouts.

The night is invading me. The light is leaving. My knees give in and I feel my body crumbling to the ground. Blackness engulfing…

"Son, are you alright?"

"Hey, can you hear me?"

"Are you alright?"

That voice. I don't want it to leave me. I burrow deeper into the voice, dive further into the blackness. But the voice is insistent. Pulls me up from the recesses of my memory.

Ajji's voice brings me from wherever it was that I had gone to. Oblivion? Death? I don't know. I open my eyes and see her face leaning over me, her worried eyes looking for signs of life. They change a bit, a little bit of that concern leaving from them.

"Ajji?"

"Are you feeling better, son?"

"Yes, Ajji. I am alright."

With a deep sigh, she sits back on her haunches and I squint for a glimpse of her face. I look for the stain between her eyebrows. It's gone, her skin is healed. Only wrinkles now. Is this now?

"You passed out a few minutes ago. Lucky for you I was sitting right there," Ajji says, and points to a temple nearby.

The wind blows through my shirt damp with sweat, sending chilly fingers of cold over my chest. I wipe my face and my eyes with my shirt sleeve. I look at the old woman again. Her face changes. So does her voice.

"Come on now. You must have passed out from exhaustion. I have a banana with me. You can eat. It will give you strength.

Then you can tell what you, a very decent-looking fellow, were doing running around in the middle of the night." She gets up and limps towards the temple.

I follow her. I feel dazed, nauseous. A burning in the pit of my stomach. I brace myself to throw up. I stop, double over, place my hands on my knees and wait. But all I manage is a belch.

"You need to drink water. Wait for a few minutes and eat something, this banana I have. You can leave when you feel a little better."

The feeble light from the lamppost behind the temple fails to reach inside. A low wall carves out a dark space around the inner sanctum. The old woman walks into the dark corridor and disappears. I strain my eyes and find her thin, skeletal figure moving in the darkness. She rests her wooden stick against the wall and, with a grunt, lowers herself to the floor.

"Come, sit. Drink this water," she says, and stretches her hand out.

My vision is blurred. I fumble in the dark, reaching out to her. My hand touches her weathered, dry arm, move up tracing for its fingers that hold a plastic bottle.

"Thank you." I take a sip of water and feel it travel down my parched throat. I slide down to the floor opposite her to see her face clearly.

"What were you running from?"

"Huh?"

"I was sleeping. Then I heard loud footsteps. I got up to see it was you, looking over your shoulder and running from what I don't know. I couldn't see anything around. You stopped midway and looked as if you had seen a ghost or something. Then you just fell to the ground, like a leaf. Did you see a ghost?" She laughs, her hand touching her nose, covering her mouth. But it is the purest sound I have heard in a while. I can feel a smile moving the muscles in my cheeks, curling wider and wider, until I can feel the wind on my gums.

"No, Ajji. I was just... just... I don't remember."

"Don't remember? You don't remember things when you are of my age. Look at you, stupid boy, you are so young. Now, tell me, what was it that scared you so much?"

"Like you said, I am still young. Young people get scared easily."

We both laugh. I take another sip of water. "You are Shantala ajji, aren't you?"

A gasp, as if wind was passing through punctured holes. "How do you know my name?" she asks.

"Do you know the woman at the lake? She told me you sit here at the temple."

"Who? Aakruti? Wait, do you hear Him too?"

Three questions. And one name. Aakruti. I feel rooted, tethered to reality. Shantala ajji named something I thought was just a figment of my imagination.

"Aakruti, yes. I met her last night. She told me you are her friend."

"Where is that stupid girl? Why hasn't she come to meet me? Poor girl, she sits all by herself by that lake, think it's some animal. Wait now, do you think it's some whale too?"

In that moment of silence when she waits for my lie, light parts the dark corner with a few thin golden brush strokes. I see her tiny head covered by the end of her green sari. Her bony index finger is curled over her lips. Her nose pin, a white, fake pearl, glitters.

"Ajji, I... I don't hear the song."

"What do you mean?"

"I have been walking in this world of Listeners as an impostor. I tell people that I hear the song. It makes me one of them. I... I want to be one with your world. But I can't hear anything. It is only silence."

She waits a long while before she replies. "Don't be hard on yourself. Everyone in this world has their path, their moment. Yours will come, trust an old woman when she tells you that. Lord Krishna will call out to you one day and you will hear the music of his flute. You seem lost. It will guide you home."

I don't want to break her illusion, I hear Aakruti's voice. I become aware of where I am, taking refuge in a world of illusions. I want to tell her it isn't Lord Krishna. It never was. Just a thing in books and a promise in afterlife we will never see. But she seems too old, too lonely to break away. Too fragile, unlike the young boy who is running away from his sins.

There are silhouettes of two idols in the inner sanctum. The light from the small lamp falls on two pairs of feet. Their faces are in a cloud of darkness. A smell of oil, fading flowers and ashes wafts through the closed space. An immersion in illusions, tangible objects to make suspension of disbelief possible.

"Does this feel like home, Ajji?"

"Yes," she says, and looks at the mute idols of Krishna and Radha, "I was once in a different home. Now, I am in His, forever. He has brought me here."

"I don't suppose you live here, do you? What about your family?"

"Family. He is my family now. And no, I don't live here. I live close by and I come here every night when I hear His music. I wait for it all day; I dream about it all day. It is the only thing that is keeping me alive. You see, that's what I am telling you. When you have nothing to live for, Lord Krishna gives you the reason."

The Lord again. But I don't feel angry or violated when I hear her talk about the Lord. I feel… I feel, sad? Maybe because I don't know what she's running away from.

"And your family?"

"I have a family. A son, his wife, and my adorable grandson, Anish. They don't live here. They moved to uh-mei-rika last year. My son, Anup, wants me to move with him too. But what will I do there? It's such a big place and all milk-white people, like ghosts. But he won't listen. No, no no. He is getting me that… what's it called? Ah, stupid old hag, doesn't remember anything."

"Visa?"

'Yes, yes. That. He has been trying to get that. It seems I can't meet him without that thing. You know, he tells me, that uh-mei-rika is very strict country. That they don't let anybody just walk into their place, especially people like me, old hags. But, before I die, I want to meet Anish once. He is just six-year-old but acts like he is a grown man." Pride takes over her voice, ebbing over her grandson's playful memories.

"I am sure you will meet him. Getting Visa isn't really that difficult nowadays," I say, and an instant feeling of regret comes over me. I shouldn't have said that.

She doesn't respond. Her laughter is gone too. Her head is turned towards the inner sanctum and I hear the rattling of her lungs. Perhaps, there are a few tears settling into her wrinkles. But I can't see them in this darkness.

"Have you been to uh-mei-rika?" she asks.

"Oh no, Ajji. I haven't."

"But you look so educated, just like my son." She is genuinely surprised. I don't know why. But I laugh before I answer.

"I don't have a job. Moreover, America isn't a place you can afford when you don't have a job. I don't think I would ever leave, even if I had a job."

"You don't have a job?" Her voice changes from astonished to confounded. "What do you do then?"

"I mean, I had a job. I used to be an engineer. I quit my job a few months ago. Now, I just… I am taking a break. I will find a job soon."

"You should. A young man like you shouldn't waste your days like a bum. Life goes by so fast that you barely remember having lived. Take it from an old woman when she tells you that. You know what, get a job in uh-mei-rika. It's such a big city, with big big buildings. All milk-white people, speaking only English. Yes, I have seen it all. Everything. My son sends me pictures and videos. You know, last time he was here, some 6-8 months ago, he bought me a phone and he did something with it. I don't know what. Now, I get these pictures and videos he sends. But, stupid woman, can't see them. Now and then, I can. But this phone is difficult." She laughs again but it's different this time, not conscious, not laughter. "Actually, it is not the phone. It is me. Halli Muduki."

Halli Muduki, it sounds like a cuss word someone has flung at her far too often until she has turned it into a label, a badge she carries on her, reminding herself that's what she is supposed to be. It is the sound of her voice, how quickly it changes, how morbid it gets when she says those words. Those two words, before silence engulfs her, and weighs down on us like the debris after a storm.

"What about your husband, Ajji?"

"That unfortunate old man passed away a few years ago. He was a good man, an honest man. Toiled in the fields all his life to build our lives. You know, he didn't want our only son to be a farmer like him. So, he put his blood, sweat and tears into his work and raised him to be an educated man. Look at him now. A farmer's son living in uh-mei-rika. I am sure he is beaming with pride right now."

"I am sure he is," I say, and wonder about the old man whose wife his son abandoned.

"I would have told you more about him but there isn't anything more to him really. He was simple man - a loving husband and a caring father who fulfilled his life's purpose and died of too much drinking or of old age or both. That's how some lives turn out to be. Simple." She yawns as if she has reminisced the simplicity of his life so many times that she is bored.

"You should get some sleep. I will walk you home, if that's okay with you," I tell her.

"Oh no. Don't trouble yourself, son. Home is here. I sleep to His music. That's the only way I can sleep now anyway. You go on, son. If you meet Aakruti, tell her to come visit me soon," she says. She reclines on the hard floor. "If it's not too much for you, come visit me tomorrow."

"I will."

I leave her at the temple and begin my walk to the lake. The night is packed with untouched quietness. And over the still waters of my mind, a memory rises like mist.

It was summer. The morning sun blazed in the dry, barren field outside Ajji's house. I sat in the veranda watching the chicken rustling through the dry leaves, looking for worms. On the trees, the leaves were dead still. From inside the house, I could hear the muffled sound of Vividh Bharati on Ajja's radio. Now and then, the sound of a peacock startled the chickens. But they soon forgot and went back to their worm hunt, and the rustling continued. In all of these sounds, Ajji's thin, soft voice was missing. But I knew she was far away, down by the river, filling the water pots for the day. And I sat there not because of the chickens or the worms or to bask in the morning sun. I was outside the house because Ajji wasn't in it.

I watched the dirt road that swept past our house. I wanted Ajji to brush my teeth and get me something to eat. There was also a growing sense of pain in my throat as if I had forgotten to swallow something I had eaten, and it was lodged in there. My lips folded and curled inwards and held between my teeth. My eyeballs hurt and jaw trembled. Then, I saw her.

She came down the road, balancing a green pot on her head. Her eyes darted downwards and watched the road. Another pot, a yellow one, rested on her waist, her left hand curled around its neck. She turned into the narrow road that led to our house. She smiled when she saw me, pushing her dark wrinkles up her cheeks. The thing in my throat exploded and my teeth let go of my lips, letting out a scream. I ran towards her.

"Putta, putta." Her voice is marked by distinctive horror. "Putta wait," she says. But I don't. I crash into her, pressing my face against her belly. The force knocks her off balance. The two pots come crashing down. They fall to the ground and the water spills out, turning the red-brown dirt darker. I jump, realizing what I had done. And I wait for a smack against my cheek. But I don't get one.

Ajji leans to the ground and holds me, wiping away my face, ruffling my hair, "Putta, what happened? Did you have the nightmares again?"

I don't remember what I said. Maybe I didn't say anything. Maybe I didn't have to say anything. With my face buried in her neck, I inhaled the smell of her sweat, the smell of the river, the smell of wood and ash, the smell of gutka.

"Come, let's get you cleaned up and get you something to eat," she said and picked up the two pots. I didn't move. I watched the muddy road. "It's alright. I will go to the river later," she said and held my hand. I felt the ring on her finger digging into my palm. I squeezed it harder and harder. Ajji didn't say a word, even if it was hurting her.

I look down at my hand and find the crushed bits of a cigarette. I search for the impression of Ajji's ring on my palm. Even if there was one, time has long erased it, just like all the other memories of Ajji. But my thoughts quickly turn as the smell of the lake reaches me. It is the closest smell to that of a river.

"Hello, Aakruti." I call out to the shadow sitting still on the shore.

"I see that you met Shantala Ajji," she says.

"How did you know that?" I ask, taking a sliver of space next to her.

"I don't remember telling you my name. No one else knows my name other than her."

"Ah, that makes sense." I smile. "Cigarette?"

For a moment, the murmur of the low wind on the water fills the space before she says, "No."

I hold the cigarette packet in my hand and realize I don't know what to do with it now. It just stays in my hand, like a dead bird. But I manage to take one out and place it between my lips. When the short flame from the lighter shoots in the air, she turns her face away, hiding her scar. But I don't blame her. It is hard to trust a man, let alone a man in the dark.

"Are you a batwoman? Out in the night, fighting crime?" I ask her.

"What?" She sounds annoyed at the possible joke.

"I am sorry. I mean, last night, you just left, disappeared without… you know, without saying goodbye. I was beginning to wonder if I had imagined you here."

"I am, unfortunately, as real as it gets. I noticed you were elsewhere. I thought you were perhaps listening to the song. I wanted to leave you to it."

The song. What would happen if she learnt the truth? That I am not one of them. I am an outsider, an impostor, an infiltrator, seeking, spying, lying, deceiving, but wanting to live amongst them. My discovery of the future is as improbable as my past.

"I… I was. True, I was elsewhere."

"Where is elsewhere?"

"My past. There isn't much left of it in my head. Just bits and pieces, scrapes of memories. I often try to put them back together to form a picture. The sight of your grandmother smiling back at you, the wagging tail of your favourite dog when it sees you stepping out of your house, the taste of mango slices you had by the street with your friends in your summer vacation, the ringing of the school bell at the end of the day and you rush out to your bicycle parked in the playground, the colour of the room where you made love for the first time…"

"What was the colour?"

"Red. It was red. Back in my college, I used to stay in a one-room flat. I had red curtains on the windows. The girl I was with then, she had come over. I remember I was sitting on the bed. It was noon. She drew the curtains and the light seeping through it, painted the whole room red. She walked up to me, her right knee rested on the bed, she kneeled over and kissed me on the lips. We had kissed before, many times. But that kiss, it was brief, momentary, like a single word uttered in silence. It was a calling, an invitation to a voyage."

A motorbike, an Enfield by the sound of it, whizzes past behind us on the road. We watch the light of many colours float on the dark waters. I pull at a blade of grass and smell it.

"Where is she now?"

"I don't know. It was a long time ago. Even that red room doesn't exist anymore. The landlord demolished it soon after I left. He built something new in its place. It only exists in my memory now. Only mine. Wherever she is, whatever room she occupies now, I am sure she has long forgotten it. Along with everything else we created back then."

"It seems like you still miss her, even though, as you say, it's been a long time."

"Miss her? I don't miss her. I remember her, now and then. For some reason, I miss that red room. I miss places more than the people. You must have such places too."

"There is. Only one. And that's the place I am going to."

"You are leaving? When?"

"Yes, I am. Whenever the whale finds me," she says. Her voice becomes one of longing, of waiting for a promise to be fulfilled.

"What do you think will happen when you find the whale?" I ask. I lean back on the grass. She joins me there. With our eyes turned to the stars, we look at the boundless emptiness that hangs above us. I imagine a whale, the largest animal on our planet, swimming in it and it looks larger than the infinite sky.

"We will climb on its back and it will ascend, beating its giant wings gently, sailing higher and higher. It will sing its song all along. Swimming through all this nothingness, it will take us to a place we always wanted to be. To a time when we never felt the need to remember, when there was nothing much to remember. And having nothing to remember, we would be free. Absolutely free from all the memories, from all the grief they bring us, from the time itself. It will take us to a place untouched by the world. It will take us to our home."

A star twinkles and then, it moves. The dead don't move. I remember the black dot on Ajji's forehead. It twinkles too. I look closer and find the star moving further and further across the sky.

"Seems like you already know where *home* is," I tell her and feel an ache permeating in my chest.

"And you don't?" she asks.

"I don't. That's why I think I will never find what I am seeking. I am a sinner, Aakruti. I have shut away something that was once, perhaps, everything for me. I suffer from the lack of its memories. But you know, when I hear a whale song, I suffer something new each time. It's as if my body, beneath this skin, harbours an array of clouds which are forever changing their shapes, to a point where they become shapeless. And a man longs for names – of people, of places, of things, of what the mind perceives. I... I just can't name these shapes inside me. It's something similar when I hear the song."

I wonder how different the song she hears is from the one I have heard in the videos. Is it more beautiful? More haunting? Truer? I try to recall the song in my head. It comes to me in bits and pieces. I try to piece them together... Has she left me again?

I turn around and see her sitting upright, staring at the lake again. The silence about her is one of reminiscence. I sit up too and wait. I didn't have to wait for long, for she turns towards me and says, "Is it too late for that cigarette?"

I hold out the packet and the lighter to her. Her hand, crawling along my arm, finds them in my palm. But she only takes the cigarette packet. I flick the switch on the lighter and the light from the flame falls on her face. I enter the dark sanctum of her eyes. Am I home?

Boo is walking on the moon. The moon is where it has always been, faraway. I take a drag on my cigarette and blow rings which float up and circle around the half-moon.

"Where is Boo?" Aakruti's voice calling out to me. "Hon, where is doggo?"

I don't say a word. I point to the moon, with my cigarette dangling between my fingers. Boo sniffs at the pole on which the American flag flutters. Boo lifts his right leg and pees on it.

"Gosh, you left the door open again." Her hand hits my arm.

"Oh, it's alright. The walk will do him good."

"Poor, old Boo. Hope he knows his way back," she says, and her head rests against my shoulder. Her left-hand wraps around my waist and her right one takes the cigarette from between my fingers.

"He is an old soul. He knows his way back. Just like I do. I always know my way back to you, no matter how far I have wandered," I tell her and kiss her on the lips. She smells of orange juice, vodka, and cigarette.

"Which reminds me, we are out of milk. Go get some now. Otherwise, no tea for you tomorrow morning. And get Boo home too." She passes the cigarette back to me.

"What? Why didn't you tell me before? It's 10:30. All the shops will be closing now."

"Well then, better hurry now, Mr. Wanderer."

A sharp knock on the door. We turn around, alarmed. Aakruti doesn't say anything. She disappears. The knocking grows louder. I *stub the cigarette in the ashtray. I look for something to wear but all the clothes have disappeared too. Even the bed is naked. Someone is breaking the door down with a hammer.*

A crack and the sunlight pours inside my bedroom. The ceiling fan spins lazily. The knocking continues.

"Yes, yes, YES," I yell. The knocking stops. I get off my bed and unlock the door.

"Oh! My god, is everything alright?" the old landlord asks, his mouth shaped in a perfect O. I am not ready for all the 'oh-s.'

"Yes, it's just, I was just feeling a little unwell."

"Oh. You look terrible," he says, his wide eyes staring at me through the thick eyeglasses.

"Thanks. But it's not as bad as it looks." I smile. "How can I help you?"

"Oh! Nothing important. I just wanted to check if everything's alright with you." He smiles back.

"Please, come in. Yes, things are fine. Why do you ask?"

"Oh, never mind that. I should be going anyhow. I just… Have you started working night shifts?"

"No."

"Oh!" Along with the smile, all the folds of skin around his mouth disappear. "Of late, I have seen you leaving your house in the night very often, almost every night, isn't it?"

"Yes, that. I haven't been able to sleep. So, I go for a walk. It calms me down."

"*Calms* you down? Oh!" he says and tries to peep inside.

"Why don't you come in?"

"No, no. I should be on my way," he says. He stops near the stairs and turns around. "Oh! Try hot milk just before you go to sleep. It helps."

"I will try that. Thanks," I say and shut the door.

The night has a way of taking you places you don't intend to go, secret whispers holding you by your hand and guiding you in the dark. I remember a story I once heard.

An old man sat at the entrance of a cave, promising treasures to the passers-by. He would convince them, one by one, sending them inside in search of infinite wealth and unbound happiness. He would sell them a matchbox, a hundred sticks in each. Each stick would last for 15 seconds. But the time to reach the far end of the cave, where the promised treasure was, took one full hour. Some men would begin their journey in darkness hoping to find their treasure in light. Others would do the opposite. But no matter how one started their journey, with light or without, there was always darkness in the end. Those who had exhausted their light, would run into each other and imagine they were monsters in that darkness. They would rip into each other's skin, filling their nails with dead flesh. Outside, the old man sat and continued to sell his matchboxes.

I had always imagined the old man with a great white beard on his face, magnificent as the sun and the stars.

I gaze at the play of light and shadows in Koramangala. I look around, not just a passing glance but with intent, as if I am in a cave looking for treasure. Maybe I am hoping to run into monsters.

I look for the stars, but they are hidden behind the thick haze of pollution that hangs above the city. The slices of the sky loom between the buildings. And a whale swims in the foul air. Its giant fins like wings, beating at the emptiness, sailing forward with soft wave-like motions. It gazes down at the city, blinking lazily at the shimmering streetlights and dark, dead windows. Its face remains unchanged as it swims and swims, with all its glorious impassiveness. It is indifferent to all those who sleep in their comfortable beds, their arms wrapped around their spouses and children. Perhaps, it's searching for something or someone out in this darkness. But I don't hear its calling, its song. I hear something else.

It sounds like the ticking of a clock. It grows louder, deliberate. It is not the sound of a hammer on a chisel. It is thinner, less violent, even soothing. I follow it and my body tugs towards the source of the sound. I enter a street and I see, up ahead, a thin man walking towards me. The walking stick in his right hand hits the road rhythmically. Tick. I wait.

The light from the streetlamp falls partially on his face, on which his cheekbones stand erect like mountains. Tick. The shadows sleep in the deep crevices of his face. Tick. His neck, long and bony, extends between a head, which looks like a shrivelled grape, tick, and a body which is thinner than the stick his arm carries. Tick.

"Who's there?" he calls out. He stops in his track.

"I… I am a Listener," I say, my tone questioning.

"A Listener?" The walking stick takes a step forward. Tick.

"Yes, a Listener. I… I hear the song, just like all the rest of you. Are you one of us?"

The walking stick stops, the man turns to stone. He looks in my direction as if he has seen a ghost. Perhaps, I have scared him. He is just a homeless old man, on his sleepless night wandering.

"I am sorry. I must have mistaken you for someone else," I say, and walk past him. As I do, I watch him closely. His body hardly twitches a muscle.

"Are you alright? You look like you have seen a ghost."

"I couldn't see a ghost, even if there was one." he says. The stick in his hand moves but hovers just an inch above the road, moving further and further until it hits the pavement. The old man lowers himself to the pavement with a groan and rests the stick over his lap.

"So, tell me about this song you hear. What do you think it is?" he asks with a practiced tone.

I sit next to him and look closely at his face. A sharp tremor washes around the hole in my chest. He hadn't seen a ghost. He hadn't seen anything, not even me. His eye lids are stitched shut, like a tear in your shirt. "Are you the one the priest was talking about?"

"Oh, you have met him? And do you still think it's some whale that's calling out to us?" He turns to me now and the light falls full on his face. He looks like a ragdoll of death.

"If you don't mind me asking, what happened to... to your..."

"It's a long story, my friend."

"It's a long night," I say and reach for the cigarettes from my pocket. "Perhaps, over a smoke or two?"

His face is turned towards me, but everything in it stays as still as a boulder on a mountain. With his eyelids stitched shut, I can't tell what he is seeing. It is like looking at the face of a sleeping man and trying to watch his dreams. And suddenly, like a ripple spreading over water, his lips curl, slow and silent, stretching farther and farther on his face until the edges of his mouth disappear in the crevices below his cheekbones. The seal of his lips breaks, revealing yellow, decaying teeth, and a sound of a maddening laughter booms out of his face, creating a discordant effect. The sound of his laughter is meatier than his face.

"I am guessing you remembered a joke about cigarettes?" I ask, half smiling myself.

"A joke, yes," he says, and falls into a coughing fit. "Indeed, a joke. I must ask you, young man. Are you real?"

"Real? Am I real? That's a question I never asked myself, to be honest. I have, on several occasions, questioned the reality of this world, of its Listeners. But never myself."

"Oh, let me answer that for you. You are real, alright. I can't possibly conjure up a man who would offer me a cigarette and ask me to tell him my story."

"So, what is it?" I ask and light my cigarette. Something tells me cigarettes come packed with history for him, not with nicotine.

"My story? Well, I will tell you, only because of what you offered in exchange. And where does one begin? Like all great tragedies, at the beginning, I suppose."

A black dog walks up to us cautiously, bowing its head. It sniffs at the old man and wags its tail. Another dog props its head from behind a pile of black garbage bags. Noticing its presence, the black dog joins it and together they begin to ruffle through the garbage.

You may look at me now and think that I am one of those ragged, defeated men. It could be true. Well, heck, it is true. I am a defeated man. Well, I used to be one. Wait, I am jumping the gun. This isn't the beginning. This is now. And for some people, now is never the beginning. I digress. I digress. Forgive me. Anyway, so.

I was born with, like they say, a silver spoon to play with. I may not be completely wrong if I told you that I might have played with airplanes made of gold. You see, my father, a giant if there ever was one, both in form and heart, was a gold merchant. His father before him. And his father before. I come from a long line of people who dirtied their hands in gold dust. I was the only child, a novel incident in the family tree. There was nothing beyond my reach. I just had to utter the word or point my fingers and there it was, whatever my heart desired. My father, not mother so much, meticulously designed a world for me where I could never learn the lack of anything. ANYTHING. And I am not just talking about things gold could buy. No, young man. I am talking about something invaluable, a father's love. He never let me out of sight. His busy world would stop, come to a screeching halt and freeze, even if I just sneezed or coughed. My childhood was one where I nonchalantly backstroked in a pool of love.

From my boyhood to teenage years, everything remained untouched, pure. My father loved me so much that not a muscle twitched in his face when I told him that I did not desire to be a gold merchant. "What is that you want?" he asked.

"An engineer. I love computers. I want to be an engineer," I said.

You know what his response was? "Which is the best college to study that?"

Ah, I miss my old man. I left home for the first time in my life and went to Delhi to study. You would think this is where my life takes a tragic turn and I learn the meaning of privation. No, sir. This is where I come into possession of two most important elements that make up the rest of my story. The first, young man, is what you are holding right now in your hand.

I don't remember when I acquired it. But it was with me when I realized I couldn't, at any cost, part ways with it. Smoking a cigarette, that anticipation when you are taking it out from the packet and placing it between your lips. That dopamine rush when you see the fire burning at its tip and when you inhale the first drag. I could feel a soothing wave passing over my temples and reaching a spot in my brain where something was waiting for that taste all along. Like a parched land waiting for rain. I smoked and I smoked and I smoked. It was especially exhilarating in the morning. You know, you have just woken up from a good night's sleep and your hands reach out to the cigarette packet lying on your table. You take the first drag of the day and everything in your life feels just right. All I remember from the first three years of my college is smoking. Alone, with friends, with chai, with beer and whiskey, at home, by the footpath, under a tree, in scorching heat, in rain, during the cold December nights. And then, I met Nidhi.

She joined my college during my final year. My junior. It did not take long for us to know that we were in love. All the awkwardness, those desperate quick glances across the hall, staying back in college long after the classes were over only to catch sight of each other in as much privacy the college could offer, those moments of embarrassment when your friends would shout out your name when she walked past you, all those childish, juvenile moments, they all passed by so quickly. But I can tell you this, young man. All the delicious stolen moments that mark the beginning of a relationship rise up to a crescendo when you have your first kiss. With Nidhi, it was the same. Everything led to that moment when I could finally embrace her, watch her lips tremble, feel my heart going mad in my chest, as I moved my own quivering lips towards hers and tasted her. The kiss lasted for, perhaps, a hundred years. But when it finally stopped, our swollen lips broke into a smile. I still remember that moment. She moved back a step, looked at me with that beautiful, soft smile, and said, "I want you to quit smoking."

I don't remember what I told her. Maybe I just smiled back, laughed, just nodded, who knows. I had just had my first kiss. Maybe I didn't register my reaction because deep inside me I could sense something. It was this weird rush of thoughts, off the leash, a stampede. Simply put, it was confusion. I couldn't understand why.

But over the next week, it cleared out. She was allergic to cigarette smoke. Well, wait. Not really. She hated the smell and, consequently, the smoker. In my case, I was an exception, in the beginning. But it had to stop if I wanted her. And of course, I wanted her. So, I made a promise to her that I would not smoke again. And with a lot of struggle and a bit of Nidhi's help, I finally quit smoking.

I will save you from all the details, which at the end of the day don't really matter much. What matters is the fact that I was deeply in love with Nidhi. I swear on my old man's grave that my love for her was pure and intense as my old man's for me. And my world would freeze when she was unwell or sad. It became my duty to shield her from the world. And soon after I got my first job, we got married.

We built a house that was designed for our hearts. A grand villa. We bought a Mercedes, black. It was her first choice. Every six months we went away to explore the world, two weeks at a time. At home and beyond, we enjoyed everything that money could buy. Between us, we savoured every little thing that love could conjure. Simply put, we had everything. We passed the initial years, together, hand in hand, without learning the meaning of the word deprivation.

Then, it was time for a get together with my college friends. We were meeting after five years or so. Seven of us, all guys, picked the best bar in Goa and began the evening of merriment. Hours rolled by, alcohol flowed like river. All the memories from our college days relived one moment after another. And somewhere in the middle of all the joyous chaos, I noticed that I was feeling a little funny in the head. I was drunk, of course. But it was unlike what alcohol makes you feel. It was different, almost nostalgic. It was then that I noticed what I was holding. A cigarette.

In all my drunkenness, I had failed to register when someone in the group had passed on a cigarette over to me. I had, maybe, taken a few drags without realizing. But this time, when I saw what was slowly burning between my fingers, I moved the cigarette to my lips and took that fateful drag. That is when I finally learnt what deprivation meant. I had everything in my life, but I finally rediscovered what I had given up, what I had let go, what I was missing without the knowledge of its absence.

It was after that party that I began to smoke again. But I hid it from Nidhi. It was my secret, a lie, a betrayal of my promise. I took all the precautions a cheating husband would take. I was good at it too. Weeks passed by. I would smoke when at work, always carried a breath freshener, a perfume bottle, and a pack of mints with me, showered as soon as I returned home. But she loved me enough to know that I wasn't my usual self anymore. The 'self' she had married. And one night, she asked, "Have you started smoking again?" Of course, I lied. Ridiculed her with my laughter. But that question, that expression she had on her face when she asked me, did not stop me from smoking. I did not quit even after it became apparent, as obvious as the sun, that I was smoking again. It was a relief of some sorts. Now, when it was all out in the open, I could smoke at home. And I did smoke at home.

Needless to say, the love between us began to dwindle. Conversations turned into arguments; arguments bred sullen bouts of silence. She tried every possible thing imaginable to make me quit again. But the reason to quit did not exist anymore. Nidhi was mine already.

When all else failed, Nidhi, my wife, my soul, finally flung something across the table for me to see. It was what started it all to begin with. Her love. Our love. What would become of her if something were to happen to me? What if I contracted cancer? What then? What would she do? What about the years we had promised to each other? Did I care about any of that?

Yes. I did. I did care about her; about the years we were yet to live. So, I tried. I tried to quit smoking again. But I guess I didn't try hard enough. It would all soon become irrelevant anyway.

The following week Nidhi complained of stomach-ache. The first night, we thought it was some gastric problem she was experiencing. But the pain persisted through the following day and we visited the hospital. Half anticipating and half giddy with excitement that we were to become parents, we reached the hospital where she was asked to undergo a series of tests. By the end of second day, our world came to a screeching halt. Time froze like a bird in a photograph. Nidhi had a terminal case of cancer.

That isn't the irony yet, my friend. Well, sure. It is some stupendous irony at this point, yes. But nothing compared to what I conjured up in the following weeks. I watched her shrivel day by day. Right before my eyes she was turning into a ghost, thinning, disappearing, growing mute. I used to pick cigarette butts; now I got to pick her failing hair. That beautiful, soft smile turned death like. Death was already inside her, eating her soul inch by inch. But at the sight of me she wouldn't stop smiling. I knew that smile wasn't an acknowledgement of my presence by her bed, by her death bed. It meant something deeper, something mischievous, something sinister. It was an accusation.

Nidhi passed away. She carried that smile, that accusation, with her till the day her lips couldn't move anymore, the same lips I had kissed, the same lips that said, "I want you to quit smoking." Yes, I had promised. And I decided to keep my promise in her death. I quit smoking. Again. But grief only grew with each passing day. Nothing could quell it. Months passed and not a day began without her dreams, not a night ended without her memory. When I couldn't take it anymore, I decided to take my own life. That would be justice. What would be more apt than dying and meeting her in heaven once again. Here I was, lonely without her. I imagined she was lonely too, without me. But I couldn't do it. I couldn't bring that knife to my veins, couldn't tie that rope around my neck, couldn't inch towards the edge of a building. Then, my mind conjured up the irony that I was just talking about. The only just way to die, the true justice lies in a death that I was promised, that Nidhi was afraid of, the death she received in the end. I would grow cancer inside me.

I picked up smoking again. And oh, how I smoked. I smoked till my tongue turned sour, dry like a sandpaper. I smoked 40-50 cigarettes a day. I smoked every waking minute. I went to bed just to keep myself from puking. And it was on one of those nights that I finally heard Death calling to me.

It began as a strange moaning, as if someone was weeping somewhere in the city, crouching in the corner of an empty room somewhere. The more I listened, the more it convinced me that it was not a person crying. It was Death. Death herself was calling out to me. It was my time; I had finally grown cancer inside me. I would meet her, embrace her and she would take me to Nidhi. Nidhi would smile and say, "I told you so." We would laugh. And together we will not be lonely anymore.

I don't know if the old man has run out of words or is lost in the memory of his dead wife. He simply stares at whatever it is that is running behind his stitched eyes. I wait. Strangely, I try to picture that beautiful, soft smile of his wife. It fails to form inside my head. Instead, something slashes across my vision, a scar. The one that is etched across Aakruti's face.

"And what happened to your eyes?" I ask.

"Oh, what was supposed to happen. A sinner pays the price, eventually. A few months ago, I was smoking and driving some place I don't remember. It doesn't matter anyway. We are always going someplace or another. The cigarette slipped my hand and fell between my thighs. I reached out to grab it and, in the process, lost control of the steering wheel. The car veered off the road and rammed into a tree. One of the branches broke and came crashing down on the car. The glass broke and a few pieces of it pierced my eyes, tearing them irrevocably. With the money that I have, I could have opted for the best surgery that was available. But I decided to keep my darkness. It was a tribute to my Nidhi, until I could see her again."

Quite an assortment of gifts for the departed – cancer, darkness, death. Or is it the demons of his addiction? His mind convincing him, serving him with a concocted reasoning so that he can smoke again. Addiction compromising with the grief. Blending in, becoming one with it.

"That must be hard on you, to relive it all. Do you want that smoke now?"

He doesn't respond. His hands tighten around the walking stick, almost breaking it. His jaw, which is already as sharp as a razor, clenches and it seems the bone would cut through his skin. He lets out a deep, long sigh and says, "I have quit."

"Oh, you have? I thought you were in a hurry to meet your wife. That righteous death you were seeking. What… what made you change your mind, if you don't mind me asking?"

"The priest," he says.

"Of course. But what did he tell *you*?" I ask, even though I am aware of the tricks.

"I was lost, and like most people who are, I wasn't aware of my predicament. My purpose, my drive to grow that cancer inside me. If I had pursued on that path any longer, I would have succeeded in meeting death. But I would never have ascended to Heaven where Nidhi awaits. I am a sinner. The priest made me see that and turned me onto a new road. My path now is that of repentance, at the end of which the Lord waits for me."

"Just like that, huh? What is that you are repenting anyway?" I ask and light another cigarette.

"I lived a life of addiction when Nidhi was alive. I was taught a lesson. Even after that, I was addicted. But this time I was addicted to death, trying to grow it inside me. Unaware of the sin I was committing, I was taking my own life. The priest enlightened me of my sin. The road to His heaven isn't one you can take whenever you wish. You have to tread the long road of life to reach there. And on this road, grief isn't salvation. The name of the Lord is."

"You no longer grieve your wife's death then? That must be awfully convenient for you, isn't it? Let me tell you what I think. You accepted the priest's words because, deep down, you wanted to live. Just like you couldn't quit smoking no matter what the cost. Even after your wife's death. You smoked because you wanted to. Not because of some great irony you thought you could conjure up. But you couldn't live with that grief at the same time. No. So, you exchanged that grief with something that gave you a new reason, a lease on a life of substitution."

"You better watch your mouth, kid," he says, but doesn't show any signs of violence other than his words and the tone in which they are uttered.

"You say you love your wife and yet, at the same time, you reduce her death to nothing more than a lesson that you needed to be taught? How is that fair to her?"

"God works in mysterious ways."

"You sound like a parrot. The professor was right. The priest is a scoundrel."

"How does that make him a bad person, if he is just helping people out of their misery? And this is coming from a man who keeps murderers for company," he says, and laughs hysterically, falling into a fit of coughing, but laughing through it, nevertheless.

"What murderer?"

"Ah, I see you are as lost as I was. Your professor, the wife killer. On the run. But not for long, you know."

The grotesque shape of the one-armed professor assumes a monstrous meaning. All those talks about the whales, the whalers, the Listeners, about love and madness and madness and love. Everything streams through my head in a whirlpool.

"Have you met him?"

"I have. And I had a similar conversation with him. But it was before I had met the priest and had learnt about his crime. Before the police learnt about his midnight wanderings. His free days are over now, you know. The priest told me that there is a policeman who wanders in the night too. It won't be long before the professor begins his tale of the whale without realizing that the Listener he thinks he is reeling in, is actually a policeman. If I were you, kid, I would stay as far away as possible from him and his experiment." He rises and his walking stick hits the road. Tick.

"What experiment?"

"I don't know. I only know that he has come to some conclusion. That John Donne was a cheat."

I am unable to build any relation between the poet and

the professor. The ticking sound of the old man's walking stick recedes into the distance, growing fainter and fainter leaving silence in its wake.

Even as I make my way to Shantala Ajji, the priest occupies my thoughts. His misplaced smile, the way it shifts in his face, grows in its significance, as if it were watching you and drawing your attention to it, while it slithers like a snake. Like his smile, the priest too has slithered into this private world of Listeners, taking away their grief and offering them his God. Each night I find a new Listener who has foregone his or her life. How long before he reaches the lake?

"Ajji?" I peek inside the temple and call out. The only light, a dim glow from a phone, disappears. There is a rustling sound, and everything goes quiet.

"Ajji, it's me. Aakruti's friend. I met you last night, remember?" I ask.

"Oh, the weak fellow. Come inside," she says, as if I were standing at the door of her home and ringing the doorbell.

We sit across from each other, as if I had never left, as if a whole day had not come between us.

"How are you, Ajji?"

"I am fine, son." She moves and groans. "Just my knees. They hurt. What else to expect at this age, no?"

"You should get it checked. I can take you to a hospital."

"Hospital? Ayyo, all these doctors are scamsters. I know what they will say. They will just diagnose and tell me I am old. As if I don't know that." She laughs, unrestrained.

"No, Ajji. They will give you pills that will help reduce the pain. You will feel better," I tell her and hesitantly add, "You should tell your son. Maybe he will come down and take you with him."

"To uh-mei-rika?" Her laughter grows hysterical. "What will I do there? I can't even read my home address properly. It's a very strict country. They don't allow illiterate people like me. They will look at me and laugh. I am just a Halli Muduki," she says. Silence fills her shadows.

I have to tread lightly. Her world is fragile. These are not her words. Whatever I might say about her son, could only make her world fall apart. Maybe she knows it, knows she has been abandoned. Maybe she's in denial.

"Son, do you know how to use this phone? In the morning it made noises when Anup sends me pictures from uh-mei-rika. But I can't find them. I used to go to Sheela, my neighbour, and she would help me. But they have all gone to their hometown. Now I can't see these pictures."

"Yes, Ajji. Let me see," I say and shuffle next to her. As I do, the fragrance of incense sticks invades me. The hole in my chest quivers. A big, clunky Vivo phone looks heavy in her shriveled hands. I unlock the phone and open WhatsApp. There's only one contact – Anup and has 36 unread messages. I click on the first one, a selfie of a man in his forties, a little kid, and a woman, huddled together in a park.

"That's my son, Anup. Ayyo, why hasn't he shaved? He looks like one gunda. That's his wife, Prerna. And that little devil you see in the middle, that's Anish. Look how he has grown. Little man boy he has become," Ajji says, her right hand covering her mouth through which her happiness exudes.

I swipe a few more pictures of the three in front of the White House, a museum, a fountain, in a restaurant and the last one at home. After we go through the pictures, I decide to teach her.

"Let me show you how to see the pictures, Ajji."

I start from unlocking the phone and lead her all the way to downloading pictures from WhatsApp. I hand over the phone to her. She unlocks it just fine. She tries, twice. But her finger freezes as if it had entered a dark room and did not know its way around. The third time she unlocks the phone, she let out a sigh and says, "Forget it, son. Now, tell me, did you tell Aakruti to come visit me?"

"I did, Ajji. I met her last night at the lake."

"Poor girl. I don't know what she suffers. All alone, without amma, appa, not even a man to console her. She doesn't care how unsafe it is out there. I have told her this. She doesn't listen. Stupid girl."

"I will tell her again, Ajji. Don't worry about her. I meet her everyday now."

"What is that you two are looking for anyway? You have your whole life in front of you. After a point, pain becomes pointless. Believe it when an old woman tells you this. After my husband died, don't you think I grieved? Of course, I did. I missed that old man everyday. I still do. Even after seven years, it breaks my heart when I think about all those years with him. But does that mean…"

"Why remember if it brings you pain?" I ask. I try not to sound desperate. My question startles her.

"What do you mean?" she asks. I can't tell if she is confused or angry.

"I mean, if memories bring grief, what's the point of them? Shouldn't one just do away with them and live?"

"Because memories make you human. There are memories which bring you joy. And there are those which make you sad.

That's what life is made of – joy and sadness. Without them, you are just a dead man walking," she says and waits for me to say something. I don't. I want her to speak.

"Let me tell you a story from my own life. When I was little, not more than six or seven years old, Amma, Appa, Akka and I used to live in our farmhouse. A small one. We were poor. Very, very poor. But we got by, you know. Amma had two goats and a buffalo. Appa would take care of the sugarcane field. Akka was older to me. She was already in school. Not like the schools you have here. Small Anganwadi, the only one in our village back then. The world was so different back then.

I had a favourite steel plate. It was small, oval shaped. I called it Appu Plate. It had a small baby elephant design on it, dancing on one leg, its small trunk curved upwards. Just above its head, the word 'Appu' was written in Kannada. Everyday Amma would serve me food in the Appu plate because she knew the plate would be licked clean. I was a fat kid because of Appu.

Then, one day, our village was flooded. It had been raining for weeks. The Krishna river overflowed into our village and we had to leave in a hurry. Appa packed all the essentials and loaded in a bullock cart and we left in search of a dry land. In all the hurry, Appa forgot to pack Appu plate. Amma kept telling me that it will be safe back at home and when we return in a few days, I could eat in that plate again. I cried a lot and waited for the rain to stop. When the sun came out and it was all bright and warm again, I couldn't wait to go back home.

After two days, when the river receded, we took the same bullock cart and went back home. But when we reached, we saw that the whole house was swept away by the river. And Appu was gone too. I cried and I cried for days. Amma beat me a few times too. Finally, hungry and tired, I ate my meals in ordinary plates.

You see? Appu is long gone. Buried under the earth or rusted, broken, turned to something new. But it's not really gone. Do you understand what I am saying? It exists in my memories. I am keeping it alive. Amma and Appa are long dead. Every time I remember it, there is this warm feeling in my heart. It's the same feeling I used to get when I would finish eating the rice and raise the plate to slurp the remaining saaru with Appu right before my eyes, smiling at me. I would smile back. This feeling will die with me. Till then, I am keeping it alive. I am keeping it alive in my memories."

"I get what you mean, Ajji. Just listening to your memories warms my heart," I say and hope she believes me.

"What are we but our stories?"

"I don't know what I am, Ajji. I have no stories."

"Maybe you are just afraid to remember them. Did something bad happen, son?" she says and sounds worried.

"That's the thing, Ajji. I don't know. It's like I have woken up from a deep sleep and all the dreams are gone. I look back and all I see is a wall," I say. Suddenly I remember a dream. "Ajji, have you seen a firefly?"

"Of course, I have, stupid boy. I grew up in a village, remember? There were so many of them. Every night, after our meal, we would go into the veranda and look out over the field. Thousands and thousands of fireflies, especially during summer. As if the night was on fire. I remember, we would chase them in the fields in the night. But crafty they were. Try how much you want, you will never get them. But why do you ask?"

"I have this dream of fireflies. I never had them before but, of late, every night, I have the same dream."

"Ayyo, something must be wrong with your eyes. Get them

checked." She breaks into a laugh again.

"Maybe," I say and laugh too, 'but, have you seen any here recently, in this city?"

"No, I haven't. But where will you find them in this city, boy? I remember seeing a few when we moved here. There is so much light now, everywhere. We killed the fireflies along with the night."

"And there is so much pollution."

"Not just that, son. We stopped looking for them. If you don't remember what you have lost, you haven't lost anything in the first place."

"Hello, Shantamma." I hear a voice, thick, tired, cold. I turn around to see a big man in khaki uniform, peeking in. A constable.

"Hey, who are you?" he asks me, and a hand rises over the half wall, and in it I see a long cane.

"Oh, leave him alone, Santosh. He is a good man. He is keeping me company and teaching me how to use my phone," Ajji says, slightly annoyed.

"Shantamma, how many times have I told you not to carry your phone with you in the night. There are thieves in this area. It's my job to protect you, you know that. You never listen. But wait, Amma, I will get to you in a minute," he says and turns to me again. "Who are you and what are you doing here?"

"I.." I stand up to show him my face. "I am just out for a walk. I can't sleep at night. So, usually walking helps. I met Ajji couple of nights back. I just come here to talk to her. Like she said, to keep her company." I smile.

He doesn't. Even though he is just a constable on a night patrol, he has an air of a military commander about him. His eyes stay locked on me for a minute. He turns to Ajji and says, "Ajji, you please come to the temple during the day. It is not safe at night. At least don't carry that expensive phone with you. How many times have I told you?"

"Ayyo, Santosh. Nothing will happen. You stop worrying. Even thieves have hearts. They wouldn't hurt an old woman like me, would they? Moreover, it is day in uh-mei-rika, no? Anup might call me any moment. I don't want to miss him."

"You don't know thieves these days, Amma. Just be careful. I must go now. But I will come see you tomorrow," he says. Before he leaves, he asks for my name and address. When asked why, he walks away without a word.

"Ajji, I think I will go too. I have…"

"I know, I know. Aakruti is waiting," she says, and laughs coyly.

"I will come tomorrow."

How long before she realizes that her son is never coming back? What would happen to her when she finally accepts the truth? I have heard of many such cases but never come face to face with someone… I love?

If you don't remember what you have lost, you haven't lost anything in the first place, her voice comes to me.

Have I abandoned my mother too?

My legs freeze in their place and I stare ahead, at the empty road, littered with patches of light between the dark spaces. I am not staring at the night but at an image superimposed over it. I see a girl in ponytails and red ribbons, sitting on the floor, eating her anna-saaru in a steel plate. She drinks the leftover saaru and looks at the dancing elephant and laughs. I see her, old now, her head veiled by the end of her sari, running her bony, weathered fingers over the plate, tracing the baby elephant, and saying in a low, soft voice, "Appu." She looks up from the plate and stares back at me with a smile. But it isn't the smile that fills the hole in my chest with that warm feeling Shantala Ajji talks about, but the black stain on her forehead.

"I am fine, Putta. It's just my knees. They hurt," she says.

I feel a heaviness in my chest, as if the hole is filling up. It isn't fear or sadness. It is… it's… it's like a well, filling with warm water. Perhaps, there is a name to it. Maybe it will come to me soon. I know what I have to do. My leaden feet begin their journey towards the lake.

"I thought you wouldn't come," I hear Aakruti's voice. I know she's smiling in that shadow she occupies.

"I… I was with Ajji." I take my place next to her. "She was talking about Appu."

"Who's Appu?"

"A baby elephant she was in love with when she was a child. I also tried teaching her how to use WhatsApp. You know, her son keeps sending her pictures. I… I never mind."

I can feel her questioning gaze piercing my shadow. "What is it?"

"I think her son is never coming back. He is lying about trying to get her a visa. He has been feeding her bullshit from there and she believes him. But I know he is embarrassed of her, wouldn't want her with him in the US. I think I will ask her to move in with me."

"Why? Is it to fill her loneliness or yours?" she asks.

"I… I don't know. Like the man with two voices says, 'together we will not be lonely anymore'," I say and smile, not at her but at my knees that are propped up to my face.

"You are a good man. There aren't many people who recognize other's loneliness. I also say that because you always have cigarettes on you."

She takes the cigarette again and waits. No matter how hard I try, the lighter switch keeps slipping from my thumb. Then, I feel her warm hand clasping mine. My thumb moves from the switch making way for her. With a single flick from her thumb, the flame burns bright. In its light, I see her face draw closer. My hand shakes violently. The grip of her hand tightens. The cigarette lights, the smell of smoke fills the air. Together, we hold onto the flame. Darker than the night, her eyes hold a question. I fail to surpass it and move deeper into them, where her sadness lies, to learn about the shape of her life. The hole in my chest wells up and warm liquid permeates every inch of my chest. I follow her pale skin, that ebbs over her cheeks, I travel further down, past her slender nose, past her thin lips, where I meet her scar. With that, the weight on my hand disappears, and the light too.

The language of words has been erased. The night cloaks us with invisibility. The distance that loomed between us, weighs down on the grass with its cavernous emptiness. Time is irrelevant. When our world by the lake pushes on us harder, there are two things which stay unruffled. The sound of her breathing and the murmur of the lake. The two blend in and become one.

The muscles in my neck twitch uncontrollably and when I finally give in and turn, I see nothing. But I hear her. I hear her breathing, the beating of her heart. They come to me soft, harmonious, like a song. Is she the song I have been searching for?

"Do you hear it?" Her voice breaks into my sanctum.

"Yes," I say. "Where is it taking you?"

"To a man. The only one I ever loved."

My bones beneath my skin crumble, one by one. My flesh thins until it becomes air. I shake free of the boulder I dragged behind me, chained to my leg. I feel a sense of freedom, but also a deep, powerful sense of melancholy even before Akruti begins to speak.

If you don't believe in God or fate, how do you assuage your frightened heart? When you believe in a creator with a grand plan, the idea that we are not in control of our lives is comforting. You tell yourself, again and again: this is how it's supposed to be, better make peace with it. That there's a bigger plan and it's all interconnected. The death of a loved one opened a new door for you, you are supposed to walk through. You assign a new meaning even to death. But none of that comes for to rescue for people like us. Death leaves a void. There is no grand plan. Never was. You live and you choose.

But we don't get to choose our parents. While growing up, my mother told me I was the luckiest child in the world because I did not have my father around. I believed her because of the stories she and her sisters told me about him. My bedtime stories were of a man, a monster that was my father. Wasn't I a lucky child? My mother assured me that the monster was elsewhere, not under my bed!

I grew up in a world of women. My mother and her three younger sisters. Later when I began to recognize words and their meaning, my mother told me stories about him. In each of these stories, he assumed a different form and shape. He was the bad wolf, a cunning fox, a witch, and an evil king. Sometimes, they didn't have to make any effort to weave him into these stories. I waited for the villain to show up and recognized him immediately. What was his crime? I was too young to understand the morality of it. But what I learned later in my life, when the toxicity of his faraway existence had seeped into my subconscious, was too simple to be true.

Mother met him when she was 19 years old. He was someone who had moved into her neighbourhood, a conservative brahmin locality. For months they exchanged fleeting glances across the street. He waited for her in his balcony and there she would be, in hers – sweeping the veranda, stepping out to buy milk, offering her evening prayers to Tulsi, hanging clothes on the clothesline. His attention became obvious, and she found new reasons to step out to allow him a glimpse of her. Days passed. The silent cues led to meetings in a nearby park. Morning walks, post dinner walks. He was everywhere, and the neighbourhood took notice. Soon the news reached home. To my mother's surprise, grandfather agreed to meet this man. And why not? He had the entry ticket; he was a brahmin too. Everything went fine until it didn't.

Mother was pregnant. The wedding ceremony had to be hurried before she showed. He said he was delighted and would bring his parents to her house the next day. Everything was going to be just fine. The next day came. And the next. And the next. Mother stepped out to clean the veranda. The balcony across the street was empty. He was gone and left no trace behind except for a letter. He wasn't ready and they had made a Mistake. Nine months later, my mother decided to give that Mistake a name. My name.

To mother's surprise, this Mistake grew up fast and fine. My mother received hate, but her Mistake was loved. My aunts doted on me. I was a gifted child. I exceled in everything I did. Everything was just fine until that day.

I still remember that day. It was summer. Schools were out. I had gathered my friends from the neighbourhood for a game of hide and seek. The seeker pressed himself against the wall and began counting. 10, 9, 8. I ran around looking for a place to hide. 7, 6, 5. Every possible place was taken. 4, 3, 2. I found a closed garage, a junkyard. 1, here I come. I managed to squeeze past the rusted door. Through the narrow opening, I peeked out. When he drew closer to the garage, I pulled back and looked around the place. I could see nothing. It was pitch black. Into that darkness, I took one step and then another. On the third step, the ground fell away from me. I pitched forward into a pile of iron rods. Many cut through my skin. But there was one which found my face and it cut deep. So deep that it would forever draw a line between me and all the men in the world.

And now, I entered my teens with a big, ugly scar on my face. It greeted people long before I did. It would always scare them away. I saw the reflection of the scar on their faces when I stood across from them and talked about the exams or a new movie I wanted to see. I wasn't talking, my scar was. They never saw the joy I had to give nor the sadness I wished to share. The boys turned away faster. I walked across the college campus and saw them sitting shoulder to shoulder with other girls. I longed to know how that felt, the warmth of their body against mine. Even the touch of their hand when they entwined their fingers with other women. Some came close but could never cross that line the scar had laid in front of me. No one stayed around me long enough to accept it. Not even mother.

She passed away when I turned 20. She was the only who came close to accepting my scar. But she failed to prepare me for the ghosts she left behind. My legacy. It was in a trunk tucked away in the attic. I found it a week after my mother was gone. In it there were many things before the Mistake. Books, magazines, unused candles, coins long obsolete, rusted jewellery boxes and an album of pictures. I recognized mother, grandma, grandpa, my aunts, uncles, and a few neighbours. There was a picture, tucked away in the last page, squeezed into the plastic sheet face down. I took it out, flipped it, and found the portrait of a man. It was the most handsome face I had seen. And from that day began a long search for that man, that stranger.

It wasn't easy. I had to start with his name, back to the landlord who rented that house to him across from grandpa's house. Further back to his college, to his friends, to his employers. I traced every step he took from that day he made the Aakruti shaped Mistake. It was like placing my finger on a map and tracing a man's journey through a hundred different towns and cities and colleges and offices, until my finger rested on his chin. When I looked up, I found myself irrevocably in love with the face my finger was pointing at. His was not the face of the monsters in mother's stories. His was not the face I had seen in my nightmares. His was not a face that looked at my scar and turned away. His eyes stayed on me and they stayed long enough to tell me that he had crossed that line that other men spurned.

He was the first man to ever look into my eyes and tell me that I reminded him of someone he was in love with. That I had a face that anyone could fall in love with. And he did fall in love with it. So, I swallowed my secret and stayed, to know what it was like being in love with a man. It was everything I had imagined it to be and more. Perhaps, it was so because I had never felt it in the first place. A woman doesn't complain about the salt water in a desert. More so when she has never known what a river tastes like.

In the quaint town of Karwar, we spent eight months savouring every inch of our soul and devouring our bodies. My skin burnt whenever he kissed it. I wasn't sure if it was because of the inherited knowledge that it was a sin or because it was drenched with pure love. If it was sin, I was the only sinner since he had no clue about my role in his life other than being his woman. If it was love, I wished everything else to be forgotten. But it wasn't easy to separate the idea of sin from love. They always came together, hand in hand, like twins in a family portrait, wearing identical frocks, hair braided in two ponytails, and carrying the same smile on their faces. Every time I saw them coming to me, I erected a wall of justifications. Who was the supreme authority on sin? The men of the world? The same men who stop short at the sight of a scar? The same men for whom the skin is more important than the soul? The same men who rape their wives and go on to seek flesh elsewhere? The man I was in love with was a man who had abandoned me. I knew that. But now that I had found him, the love he showered made up for all his years of absence. I forego his mistake. I let go of myself. To him. I was with a man in a room. I would look at him and paint a stranger. I would assemble him, piece by piece - his name, the beard on his face, the colour of his shirt, the scent of his neck, the curve of his smile, and the hardness of his cock. I shut my mother out every time he undressed me. Every time he slid inside me, I wrenched him from his past and, with my legs wrapped around his naked body, I held him for what he was to me in that moment – a man making love to a woman.

I worried about what would happen to us. Would our past ever forget us and leave us be? Will I ever be able to change the blood that was running inside me? Sooner or later my past would catch up with me and consume him. Contrary to the monster in my mother's stories, he was a good man. He made a Mistake when he was young and did not have the strength to face it. His past had crept up on him without his knowledge. It was only a matter of time before it destroyed him. And destroy it did.

I constructed a perfectly fabricated past for myself. I

remember the evening I presented this to him. We were sitting by the beach, gazing at the water. Just like we are doing now by the lake. I started with the names of my dead parents. Along with those, I changed the names of schools and colleges I studied. I borrowed from other lives I had known. Friends and relatives as fictional as the idea of sin. The story was woven to keep myself around him.

And all it took was a single photograph to disintegrate everything I had built, everything we had built. His own picture that I had tucked away in my belongings in the deep folds of my real past. I could hear the shattering of a life when I found him, kneeling on the floor, holding the portrait of his younger self in his hands. He killed himself the following day.

When I emerged from that world we had built, the world outside was waiting. Sometimes I think death did him a favour, taking him away before the world broke him. I was left behind for that. To add to the world's glee, I was a woman. The sin of incest that my lovestruck mind had deconstructed lay in pieces before the world, to be picked up and hurled at me wherever I went. I dodged their beating for a whole year until I couldn't anymore. I came here, to this city, to lose myself in its multitude and become a stranger again, to myself, to others. But the whale knows who I was. It sings to me the song of my past, reminding me not of my sin but the love I had for him.

When the waves of her past had subsided, the murmur of the lake filled the silence left behind by her voice. I receded into myself and wandered the vast caverns inside me. I looked for anything that would help me measure either the love or the sin Aakruti had committed. But these caverns were as empty as my past. Empty white walls waiting for an occupant.

"You are not afraid of my scar. But if my past scares you, I understand."

"It doesn't. Both your scar and your past have brought you here and I am glad I met you."

My hand that rests on the grass is touched by a familiar warmth. In the little space that separates us, our hands hold each other, our fingers entwine, and fill the empty spaces in us. I feel a sudden shudder of violence in my body. The void inside my chest, collapses onto itself and a sound emerges. It takes me a while to recognize its rhythm, the steady beating.

Hello, my old friend!

"What are we watching?" Aakruti asks, placing the bowl of chips on the table. She goes back to the kitchen. "Beer?"

"Yeah," I call from the couch, browsing apps on the television.

"So, what are we watching?" she asks again. She passes a beer bottle and settles down beside me.

"You choose," I say, and clink her bottle. "Cheers."

I place the beer to my lips when she shouts, "Wait. What are you doing?"

"What?"

"You are supposed to look into each other's eyes when you take the first sip. Otherwise, you will have a bad sex life."

"Alright, you pervert," I say and we both take our sips looking at each other. "How about we skip the watching and get down to it?"

"Here? On the couch?" she asks.

"Yeah, why not?"

"Ajji might walk in on us."

Has the night changed its colour? The shadows lingering at the corners of the streets, now seem different. As if they are worn out, like the colour of a red car that has been left out in the sun for too long. Since the time I have left my house, I look at the streetlamps and wonder if they are brighter now, and hence the shadows less dark. But I know they aren't.

There's been a storm raging inside me the last few nights. Uprooting all the graves from which long dead friends have returned. I have been curious, angry, afraid, sad. All these wore new faces, but I could still recognize them for who they were. But ever since her hand sought mine in the darkness by the lake, I feel like I am going to crack open, like an egg. Who will I be?

The question blows away the mirage of thoughts, and there emerges the face of the sculptor. I feel a stabbing pain in my chest, as if my heart was screaming and the muscles in its throat were tearing apart one by one. But as swiftly the face emerges, it evaporates like the smoke from my cigarette. When it clears, I find myself in an unknown street.

I am not where I am supposed to be. The houses on the right side of the road are quiet, asleep with faint square light carved at their windows. The big, tall trees next to each of them, watch me in silence, as if I were a stranger in their garden. On the left side, there is nothing, just a vast pool of darkness. I stare at it, wondering if I were standing at the edge of the universe and peering into the void beyond. It reminds me of the abyss next to my house. The memory of the dot of light shines bright in my mind and I stand in absolute silence, gazing into the abyss.

I hear the song.

It's faint, weak, and comes to me from a vast distance. A long wailing sound, broken in places by clicks and clacks. When the short noises disappear, the wailing continues, as if the whale is wounded. The more I listen, the more I know it's calling out to me. And without my consent, my legs move, and I enter the abyss.

I follow the sound. It's everywhere in the abyss. The song grows louder and then recedes into the distance. With my arms outstretched I walk on, feeling the stony ground below, afraid I will tumble and fall into a bottomless pit. The fear is palpable in my heart. The song grows nearer and nearer. I follow the song. I am a blind man walking in the darkness. My hands beat at this darkness for something to hold onto. And just then the song dies. Silence takes away the only sense that was guiding me. Fear surges in my veins and I run frantically, hoping to find something, anything. My body crashes into something warm, something alive.

"Wh.. who are you?" I shout.

"What are you doing here?" A voice, coarse, shredded, shouts back.

I realize the man is afraid too. He isn't a monster in the cave of the old man with the great white beard. He is merely lost, like me. But something about his voice feels familiar. Like listening to the voice of a friend over phone with bad reception.

"I heard the song. I was only following it. Who are you?" I say, and then it becomes apparent in an instant. "Wait. Were you the one singing?"

"Yes, of course. Until you came along and interfered in my search," he says.

"What are you searching for in this pitch-black darkness?"

"What? The whale, of course. What is wrong with you?" He seems annoyed as if I had asked a very stupid question.

"Why were *you* singing like... like a whale?"

"What do you think the whales are doing when they sing? They are searching. But not for food. No. No. No. It sings for a Listener. The song is meant for this *other*. Someone, anyone. The song is nothing but a calling. So, you see," he says with a short laugh, "I am fooling it into believing that I am a whale too. That I am seeking it in return. Soon enough it will find me, and I will find it and together we will not be lonely anymore."

His laughter is broken in many places. Through its cracks, I hear the sound of his loneliness pouring out.

"And you think it can hear this song of yours?" I ask, but the question, in parts, is thrown inward.

"This is my song, yes. All the Listeners of the night are singing in their own way. But the world cannot hear our song anymore. Our song is broken. The world's ears don't recognize it anymore. To them, our wailing is silence, over which their music ebbs and drowns us. And way beneath, where the abyss is, we swim alone, singing our song, looking for a Listener who can hear it. I will find the whale soon and together we will not be lonely anymore."

In the vast open space, the wind blows freely. I look straight ahead, hoping that's where the stranger is. "I have been part of this world since a week, and I have met many Listeners but I still don't hear the song. Neither do I have a song to sing. What does that make me?"

"Not one of us," he says.

I am an intruder. I am an outsider to the world of light, and an intruder to the world of Listeners. The answers burst inside me like kernel.

"But I want to be one amongst you," I say, my voice desperate.

Nothing.

He is gone. Faraway, in the distance, the wailing of the man resumes.

I pick a direction and begin walking. It doesn't matter if my eyes are open or closed. It makes no difference. I am not afraid but ashamed. Ashamed of my intrusion. Ashamed of letting Aakruti's hand touch me. But how does it matter who I am as long as I am there for her? Doesn't matter. Doesn't matter. It does. It does. Because she held the hands of a man who, she thinks shares the same fate as she does. You don't. You don't share anything, neither with the world of light nor with the world of Listeners. And that's why you can't hear the song. You are doomed. Forever doomed. There is no saving for some people. What do you want to be saved from anyway? A past you don't remember? Suffering you don't feel? Loneliness that wasn't felt all these years? You are a dead man walking. And you keep walking until the ground beneath you gives away and you fall into your grave. Your death is your only freedom. Kill yourself and be done with all this fucking bullshit. At least you were better off when you were all alone, just drinking, smoking, twitching like a dying fish. Now, look at you. Pathetic. Fuck this world of Listeners and wailers.

I see the dead buildings and the veil of light on them. The voice inside me dies a sudden death. I am afraid it will find me again. And I feel an urge to sleep. But I can't. Not until I have met them again.

Only a few moments ago, I had it all figured out. Whether I hear the whale or not, it doesn't matter. What matters is that I gather the two people who matter the most to me now. Hold their hands and walk out of everything. Walk to the light, build a home, build a life and never look back. Heal. Together we will not lonely anymore.

I will ask Ajji to move in with me. I can take care of her. She doesn't have to worry anymore, neither of her son abandoning her nor of her aching knees. She doesn't have to fret over what would happen to her. I will provide everything she needs. She can recline in her armchair and spend her warm afternoons remembering her old man, her favourite elephant, and she can tell me about the fireflies.

The temple looms into the view. My heart races as I approach it. My palms begin to sweat. I rub them against my pants, take a deep breath, and walk inside.

"Ajji, are you still awake?" I look towards her spot. The shadows have thinned, and I can see her better. Her white-pearl nose-pin shimmers to greet me.

"I was waiting for you only. Come, come. I have good news," she says. Her joy is palpable in her voice.

"What is it, Ajji?" I ask, taking my seat next to her.

"Anup called me a few hours ago. He left the job and is moving back to India. He said he will be here next month. He has already asked someone to search for a bigger house where we all can stay together. One bedroom just for me. Oh! I can't wait to meet the little brat Anish. Now I don't have to feel content just by looking at his pictures. I told you, this WhatsApp is useless for me."

She doesn't know the happiness in her voice makes a mockery of my dreams. She clasps her hand and bows to the Lord. "Krishna! I knew you would take care of my wishes. I knew you would take care of me."

She is waiting for my reaction. "That is good news," I tell her. "So, does that mean no more late-night temple visits for you?" I chuckle.

"I will visit Krishna till my son is back. After that, do you think he will allow me to step out of the house in the middle of the night?" She laughs. "As it is he worries too much about me."

Worries too much about you? He abandoned you all these years. Now, he decides to come back? You will be nothing more than a nanny to his kid. He doesn't worry about you. He doesn't care. I did. How could you not see that? Why did you have to go ahead and betray me like that?

"That is good news, Ajji," I say and stand up. "I have to get going now."

"Oh!" she says, and after a brief pause, she lets me go. "Alright, son."

She's looking at me. But I can't see if she's smiling, sad or just indifferent. All these moments, and I still couldn't penetrate the final layer of shadow in which she always sits. All the words have lost their significance here. We just stare at each other in silence. She doesn't stop me. It is simple. I do not matter anymore. Never did, maybe.

Did my mother abandon me even before I could see her face?

The heaviness in my chest weighs down my legs. I shuffle as I walk, as though I have been on a long arduous journey and am looking for a place to rest. But I know the destination isn't far. I just have to cover this lonely road, where the shadows watch me from the corners they have receded to, until I reach the lake. Aakruti will be waiting for me. I know. She may never un-love the man. But she may love me. That's enough. I will take anything she has to offer. We will find our own place in the day. And together, we will not be lonely anymore.

I hear the tapping of the stick up ahead. A man emerges under the light from the lamppost. Santosh. The policeman. He is walking towards me and sees me too, and the cane in his hands stiffens in the air, just above the ground. As he approaches, I look at his face to see if he recognizes me. There is no smile but there's an acknowledgement. His eyes stay fixed on mine, as we walk past each other. I wonder if I should stop him and give him the good news. I don't. I walk on without turning.

The air around the lake is colder tonight. There's a soft breeze too. I squeeze through the narrow opening in the fence and climb up the grassy mound.

"I have some good news," I call out to Aakruti. Her silhouette, etched against the softly lit lake, shifts in its place.

"Yeah? What's that?" Her voice has a tinge of excitement.

"The prodigal son returns," I say, and take my seat next to her, this time without measuring the space.

"You mean, Shantala Ajji's son?"

"Yup. Coming back next month. Most probably laid off is my guess," I say trying hard not to sound affected. "Ajji seems happy though. So, that's that."

She turns towards the lake and gazes at it in silence. "You seem unhappy about it," she says.

"I am not unhappy. I am just... I thought..."

"I know. But life is cruel, even when it's kind." Her hand brushes my arm briefly. I fear life is watching me.

I chuckle. It dissipates my fear for the moment. And then I fight this insatiable urge to see her face. To look into her eyes and see if she's lonely. I am not. Not at this moment. I hope she sees it too in my eyes. I hope she sees the reason. I hope the light from my lighter is sufficient for her to see her reflection in them. Life will be watching us, I know that. I only hope it sees two people sitting by the lake, huddled around the light of a firefly.

"Aakruti, have you seen a firefly?" I ask her.

The sharpness of her laughter, the cackles that pour out of her mouth, ebbs over the murmuring of the lake. I feel stupid and happy.

"Fireflies? What made you think of them?" she asks.

I laugh, too. "You know how sometimes you can't separate dreams from your memories? I dream of fireflies. I have never seen one. At least I don't remember seeing one. And that's what troubles me because I know you don't dream of anything that isn't part of your subconscious. I suppose I have buried those fireflies deep within myself, for reasons I don't recall. Of late, they are beginning to glow and I see them but only in my dreams."

"You don't remember anything? Not even your parents?"

"I grew up with my grandparents. Ajji used to tell me that my parents passed away when I was just an infant. But something tells me that's not the whole truth. Maybe she lied to me since I was a sick child. I have spent more time in hospitals than I have in schools…"

"What sickness?"

"It wasn't any particular disease. I used to just randomly fall asleep a lot, it seems. At least that's what Ajji used to tell me when I asked her about the hospital visits."

"Do you mean blackouts? Did you pass out?"

"I guess. I don't know, really. I was too young to remember anything. I remember things from the time I stopped going to the hospitals. I was maybe 9 or 10. Like I remember the house we used to live in. A small hut. It was in the middle of a field. We had chickens and some goats. Most of my memories are about Ajji. Sometimes I would accompany her to the river to fill drinking water. I remember the time our village used to get flooded by the river and we would go packing until it receded. Once, there was a rumour of some villagers spotting a giant creature in the river and for days no one would go near it. I remember the black patch on Ajji's forehead that kept growing and growing until her whole face had turned into a shadow of itself. And that's the thing. I remember all those things I shared with Ajji, but none about seeing fireflies that I dream about these days." I take a moment when I realise something. "You know what, Aakruti? This is first time I have actually spoken about it to anyone."

"That's what's important, isn't it? To talk. When you are narrating your life to someone, you are recording your own life. Sharing memories is chronicling life. Memories, even if they bring you grief, is how you keep your loved ones alive, your past alive."

"I suppose it is. But you also need a listener, don't you? The pubs are awful loud in this city."

"Yes, but the lakes are quiet," she says and holds on to her words for a moment. "Do you know how to swim?"

"To swim? Yes, I do. I used to go swimming all the time in the river when I was a teenager."

"That's nice," she says, and it feels like she's speaking to me from a distance. "I never learnt swimming. Sometimes, when I sit here and hear the whale, I want to walk into the lake and sink deeper and deeper, till I find the whale that's waiting for me."

"But that would kill you."

"At this point, it doesn't matter what happens to me. I just…

just want it to hear me and find me."

and you would climb over it and it would take you faraway

Where skin isn't the measure of your soul

Where sadness isn't a sin

Where you can touch your lover and not just his souvenirs

Where we would smell the time when it smelt of rain

and where the fireflies come out in the summer heat

and when in winter, you can reach out your hand for the warmth of your lover's body

You can hear your name in her voice

Where we would smell the wind when it smelled of new, unheard poems

We would taste the words spoken without cigarettes

We would hear the call of memories, bitter and sweet

We would hear the sounds of all that's in-between

And where, together, we will not be lonely anymore

"And what if you are wrong?" A familiar voice breaks into our reminiscence.

We turn around and see two silhouettes carved in the faint light from the road behind them. Towering on a mound, they stay still, looking towards us. We rise up, alarmed. I know who the voice belongs to. I try to recognize the other silhouette. It isn't hard. The man on the right holds a walking stick. As I had feared, they have reached the lake.

"What do you want?" I ask.

"There is no need to be afraid. I know how it looks. The sight of two men in the middle of the night is scary, especially for a woman. I apologize for walking in unannounced. We mean no harm. We are the messengers of the Lord."

The shape of the words and the tone in which they are carved, makes it hard to believe. His voice is ominous.

"We are not interested in the message," I tell him, trying to sound stern.

"Would you rather be misguided that it is some song of a creature?"

"It is what it is. Now please leave us alone."

"I am not here to ridicule what you believe in. Trust me. And I will leave. But before I do, let me ask you something. Have you heard of Pascal's wager?" he asks, and strangely the sound of his voice is disarming.

"Enlighten us," Aakruti says and takes a step forward.

"It's a theory. It says, one should live their lives as though God exists. If you are a rational person, you will find merit in this argument. If it turns out that God doesn't exist, you have nothing to lose once you die. But, if He does, and you lived as though He didn't, you only end up with eternal suffering. Think about it. Now, I will leave you two. I will come back some other time for your answers. Like I said, I mean no harm." With that, he gathers his bettors and leaves.

I let out a sigh of relief. I hear my heart slowing down. Strangely, Aakruti is calm.

"Would you rather take the bet?" she asks.

"What bet?"

"Believing."

"But I do believe. Just not in their version of what the song is. Would you take the bet?"

"Too old and tired to be bullied into believing. If it wasn't a priest, it would have been some other holy man from some other faith, telling you what the song means. Why would I bet on his Lord when there are million others? Allah, Krishna, whatever. All equally impossible. You pick any, you are already gambling. I would rather live and grieve what I know here, on this earth, with the people I love, however sinful it may seem to others."

A strange silence flows after her voice. In it, we float like two whales in an endless sea. It is all around us. It has seeped in us and washed away all the words. Our bodies twitch and before we realize, they hush the twitching with a warm embrace.

She lifts her head, and I can feel the warmth of her breath brushing against the tip of my nose and my lips. My hands travel up and cradle the back of her neck. And in that darkness, I taste her.

With our lips gripping each other, her unspoken words travel into me and mine into her. It's a declaration made in silence. A point of no return. I am holding Aakruti in my arms that have stopped trembling. The certainty of her body clasped in my arms dissolves all the abstraction inside me.

I watch as our bodies, without our consent, move. We descend to the ground, on the cold blades of grass. My lips leave hers and they search for the scar on her face. I feel its coarseness, lick it. Her hands let go of my hair and travel over my back. They search for my skin under my shirt. I feel them burning on my back. I bury my face in her neck, kissing, nibbling, breathing in all of her. Her hands unzip my pants and reach for my dick. It burns as she grips it. I let out a moan and the grip tightens. But they leave me for now and get busy undressing. I touch her between her thighs and it's as wet as the lake. Her left-hand presses against my chest. I stop and stare at her in that darkness. I can see her clearly. I wait. Her lips find mine again. And in that moment, her right hand holds me and guides me into her. I push. Her lips tear away from mine, and I hear a soft moan escaping her mouth.

"There… do you hear it too? The song?" she asks, her voice trembling.

"Yes, yes I do," I lie and sink deeper and deeper.

"It's been 14 days. I think we can do it," Aakruti says, cutting her steak with the knife.

"Urgh. I don't think I can," I say and take a sip of wine. "Drinking only makes me want to smoke more."

"Come now. You aren't going to start again. This is what we wanted. We promised each other." She looks over her plate, her jaw working on the steak.

"I know, I know," I say, and smile.

"What the fuck is this?" a loud voice asks.

I turn around and see a man, bare chested, sitting at a table and shouting at the waiter. "What is this green shit? You think I am going to eat whatever the fuck you serve me here and quietly pay you 1500 bucks for a steak?"

Aakruti has suddenly gone quiet. Her hands trembling, teeth grinding, wide eyes, nostrils flaring.

"Hey, hey. Aakruti. Easy now. The manager will handle it," I say.

"You cannot yell at the waiters. Entitled assholes," she says, and begins to foam at the mouth, her skin turning purple.

"Hey, listen," I place my hand on her arm. "It's the management problem. They will handle it. Why should we get in trouble?"

She looks up at me and says, "I know, but…"

A tap on my shoulder. I turn around to face a fat man standing next to me. "Sir, this is inappropriate. I will have to ask you to leave."

I look down at my limp dick.

It's as if I woke up today and could name the hours, infuse them with a sense of movement. And I have been on the move ever since. All these nights, it was as though my feet couldn't carry the heaviness in my chest. Tonight, I walk the street with a lighter heart. My feet do not move until I decide the direction. And I decide to take the quickest way to the lake.

This too shall pass. Graffiti painted in black on the compound wall. My heart wants to believe in it. I found Aakruti when I was seeking a whale. Finding a job and a house should be easier than that. All these wanderings will pass, and I will find myself in the light again. I remember seeing the same graffiti on the night I stepped out with Aakash. Life comes full circle; I chuckle and kick a stone. I watch it roll on down the road, disappearing in the brief shadows before slowing down at the distance and finally coming to a halt. The sound of the rolling stone has alarmed a man up ahead. He stops in his path, taking refuge in the darkness between the two lampposts. I see his silhouette swaying gently. A drunk man. He watches me for a moment and resumes walking. I notice the incompleteness of the silhouette. I recognize the missing piece. I run to catch up with the professor.

I call out, but it's too late. He turns to his left and disappears into a narrow gully. Déjà vu. A familiar moment. I turn into the gully to find him sitting on a pile of stones, gasping for breath. He takes out a cigarette and lights it.

"Cigarette?" he asks, offering me the cigarette packet. His hands shake uncontrollably.

I perch on stones next to him and light my own cigarette. We smoke in silence and catch our breath. Although it wasn't a long distance, my body bleeds sweat.

"I thought you were a cop or something," he says with a chuckle.

"Yeah, I heard about it. You are famous," I say and echo his chuckle.

"The quickest way to fame is crime. Not good deeds. To be known for good deeds, you have to be good for a long time. It's tough work."

"It was hard for me to believe you are a criminal. Maybe I am foolish and slow," I say.

His body sways, lightheaded with the nicotine rush.

He lets out a short laugh, controlled, deliberate. "You may be foolish and slow. But you are not blind," he says. He takes a deep drag. "I suppose you want to know about my crime?"

"Every single detail," I say.

His head hangs low, and he gazes at his feet, where his toe wiggles in his worn-out sandals. He flings the cigarette butt over his shoulder and lights another. Without turning to me he begins.

I was a professor of anthropology. I was quite young myself when I began teaching post-grad students. Difficult as it may be to believe now, I was a nice, polite man in a position of authority given to me by the college. They were young brats with their own authority of youth. They were quick to spot my softness and quicker still to misuse it. Pieces of chalk would come flying towards me whenever I turned to the board. The murmur from the back benches never ceased, despite my constant pleading and warnings. I would stand closer to the first few benches where my brightest, obedient students sat, so that they could hear me.

I would be teaching them about different schools of thoughts, when some of the back benchers, without acknowledging my presence, would walk out of the class. Back then students would skip classes and go to movies, you know. Drinking was not common. Anyway, I would call out to them, but my meek voice would fail to stop them. Those who stayed behind for whatever reasons, would crack up and laugh at me, staring right in my face. But my classes went on with a few students who took interest. And like all cliched stories there was a girl, a student in my class, who was interested in more than what I had to teach. She was shy, pretty, and a studious girl. Jyoti would linger long after the class was over and hang around the faculty office aimlessly. She came up with the flimsiest excuses to strike up a private conversation. Gradually her presence grew on me and we started seeing each other. In secret, of course.

"You have to be stern." Jyoti lectured me whenever we met. "You cannot let them bully you. You cannot be nice all the time."

I nodded, embarrassed, and whipped. Back home, I stood in front of the mirror and practiced my meanness. "Get your ass back in your seat," I yelled but I wasn't really screaming at my reflection. I was screaming at myself. As if all the pent-up anger inside me had finally found ways to pour out. It was intoxicating.

Do you know the poem '*No man is an island*' by John Donne? I was obsessed with it then. I read and thought about it every single day. Not only because of its turn of phrases, the structure, the rhythm, but by the questions it evoked. Could a man ever be an island? Could a man be an island and be free from all the bonding? Or are we all forever connected? These connections which bring happiness and joy and sorrow and misery and heartaches? Back in those days, obsessed with the poem as I was, I believed that no man could survive all by himself, no matter how isolated one is, a man can never be alone and thrive and create happiness.

If I remember it correctly, I think I was teaching my students about Antihumanism. On that day, I recited the poem in class, and I wrote the question *'Can a man be an island?'* on the blackboard and had left it as is. The following day someone had added two words to my question. It now read *Can a man be an island of farts?* I did not have to summon my practiced meanness. It was there, lurking below the surface.

I asked the four boys, the back benchers, if they wrote it. They laughed. A response which was neither a denial nor acceptance, but a mockery of my question, of me. I suspended them for a month. They brought their parents. I told them about the nature of their kids outside home. Failed them the following month in the mid-term exams. I even sought opportunities where I could punish them. Finally, they were on their knees, begging for mercy. They did that in private. But I wasn't satisfied. For ten whole sessions, they had to kneel in front of the class, while I taught about gender roles. The feeling of power and rage was intoxicating. I had changed. All it took were a few words from the girl I was in love with - *you can't be nice all the time*. I stopped being nice all the time.

A year later, when my class graduated, I married Jyoti. We were good together. Had a happy marriage. Of course, there were those occasional fights that are part of one's shared life. After all, we both agreed that we can't be nice all the time. She had taught me that. It is not human at all. In that way, we understood each other better than most couples in their marriages. As the cliché goes, we were perfect for each other. And the years passed, all uneventful except one.

Five years into the marriage, our child passed. Dead on arrival, doc said. Not in those words, of course. I don't remember what happened in the years that followed. It's all hazy. I guess

Jyoti and I just sort of survived through the grief. When we emerged on the other side, there was one thing that had changed and would undo our lives. In grief, she had found religion.

Jyoti was never a religious person. She didn't care for festivals or God or His benevolence. That's what I, always an atheist, loved about her. We were nice to each other because of the love we had, not because some book told us to be so. Religion was an act we put up for her parents.

In those hazy years of mourning our unborn child, something was working in the darkness, in all the quietness that we both shared. Jyoti was undergoing a strange, silent transformation. This metamorphosis of Jyoti would soon become apparent.

I began to notice her praying to the idols in private. We did have a few idols for when her mother, a staunch brahmin, visited. Jyoti's favourite Agatha Christie novels were replaced by Bhagvad Gita. Walls changed their skins and now donned posters of gods and goddesses. There was a constant fragrance of incense sticks wafting through the house. She attended the religious ceremonies in the neighbourhood temples. I watched it all from a distance. I did not question her. If she had found peace in it, strength to cope with the grief of being childless, I wouldn't come in her way with my rationality. That would be mean.

But her devotion to a benevolent God and the wisdom of her holy books did not stop with her prayers. It began trickling into our shared lives.

I remember the evening I returned home earlier than usual. My mind was preoccupied with the thought of one of my good students caught hanging out with bad company, smoking weed in college. I sat in front of the television and watched the news about the beheading over cartoons of a prophet. My thoughts swayed back to the poem. Is this how we are all connected?

Fighting over long dead prophets and cows? Jyoti sat next to me and talked about a cat which had entered the kitchen and spilled the milk. I nodded absent-mindedly, my thoughts still on this new interpretation of the poem. She stopped speaking, and a moment later, she uttered two words in her gravest tone, "Be nice." I let go of my thoughts and I listened to her prattle.

There is a special kind of evil in good. A good heart can be cruel. It thinks it is capable of changing anything, that it deserves the change because it is good. It owes this goodness to itself. It is intoxicated by its own self-righteousness and a heightened sense of morality.

Jyoti always had a good heart. Now her heart expected goodness in return all the time. I was once in her place. I was a good man who was never unkind. But the world did not treat me the same way in return. Instead, it taught me, Jyoti taught me, that's not how it works. You cannot be nice all the time. But I tried.

I tiptoed around her feelings. I measured my words, my gestures, my attention, and even my love. I watched my words and behaviour, both inside and outside the house. But there were moments I would slip and a harsh word or an inattentive gesture would catch her eyes and ears. She wasn't mean to me in return. Instead, she only had one response. Be nice.

Those two words – Be Nice - she would slide them across the room, towards me, like a dealer sliding two cards across the table. Be. Nice. Slow, calculated, with measured tone and pace, calm and with a tinge of authority. And with that, the language between us began deteriorating, both of words and touch. The goodness of God began to rule over us through her. It was a reign of unabashed morality.

I remember once we were out in the garden, talking to our new neighbour across the compound. I don't remember how but we arrived at this topic of politics. The man, a staunch nationalist, said, "These liberals must be taught a lesson."

"Who are these liberals?" I asked.

"You know, those who question every little thing our government does and raise slogans and hashtags."

"And questioning those elected to serve us is a bad thing?"

"Of course, it is. How can they not know the government does what's best for the common folks?"

"What makes you so sure?" I asked, my tone questioning and stern.

But then, I didn't have to wait for his response. Jyoti intervened, chiding me with those two words, "Akumal, be nice." I looked at her, unsure, perplexed. I knew she meant "be nice to the new neighbours". But I couldn't understand what was so mean about what I had asked. I turned to the man, who wore a sorry smile, as if I was ignorant and to be pitied. I, a professor, who had studied and taught subjects on society and morality, on good and evil, I was being pitied and whipped at the same time.

Those two words stuck with me like weak knees in old age. Wherever I went, whatever I did, I heard them in her voice, as if I were a wayward kid. Those two words reminded me that I was not good enough, that I was lesser of a human. She demanded unconditional goodness from me because she had turned good herself. 'But you should do this because this is right', 'but, you can't do that because that is wrong', 'God keeps a count of everything', 'You are being mean'. Like I said, a good heart is cruel in its own special way. I had become a slave to her goodness.

There was no escaping it. After a few years, it wore me down. I was tired of being good, tired of everything around me. I saw good in evil and evil in good. And after a point, everything became abstract. I felt suffocated. I wanted to run away from all that. It was then that the poem came to my rescue. My old fascination for its answers.

No man is an island,

Entire of itself,

Every man is a piece of the continent,

A part of the main.

If a clod be washed away by the sea,

Europe is the less.

As well as if a promontory were.

As well as if a manor of thy friend's

Or of thine own were:

Any man's death diminishes me,

Because I am involved in mankind,

And therefore never send to know for whom the bell tolls;

It tolls for thee.

So, I started questioning. Can a man be an island? Free from all that binds him? The good? The bad? These subtle sorrows, these mighty miseries? I began to question John Donne's authority over human nature. What gave him the special place to pass judgement on all of human nature? I would prove him wrong. I would prove that John Donne was a cheat.

I began testing my theory in a slow, but meticulous fashion. I started by disassociating myself from everything. I quit my Bookworms' Club, stopped speaking to my friends and colleagues, even estranged myself from my mother and brother. I watched myself as if under a microscope, noticing subtle but evident variations in self. It felt like I was walking away from a battlefield, felt at peace, happy even. But I couldn't cut myself away from my wife. She was always after me with a saw of goodness, chopping me here and there, trying to create a perfect piece of furniture, if you will. I was hoping to shed everything and walk away. Instead, I found another man growing inside me, a man full of hate and poison which my wife nourished blindly with all her goodness. She had turned me into an evil man. This man wanted to break free and become an island.

It wasn't planned. But it happened, nevertheless. There is no escaping from that. I was sitting and writing down an essay on this new theory of my own. Jyoti walked into the room.

"I want you to light deepa and offer prayers," she said.

"What?"

"I have my periods. So, I cannot perform the rituals. You should do that for the next three days."

"I can't. I am busy."

"It will take you ten minutes," she said.

"It isn't really about time."

"Then what is it about? You did that for me all these years."

I turned to her, looked into her eyes and said, "I can't do that anymore. I did that out of fear. I have had enough. I am not afraid of your goodness anymore. If your Lord is good enough, he will surely forgive a devotee praying during her periods. Unless, of course, he thinks it smells."

"Be. Nice," she said.

I walked up to her and said, "No."

"You are being mean."

The word 'mean' rang in my ears like a gong hammered

unannounced. All the meanness that I had stored and locked away all those years burst open all at once.

"I was good once. You taught me about the good in evil, in meanness. Now that you have borrowed your goodness from your damn books and prayers, you expect me to change myself once again? Fuck you and fuck your God."

"Akumal, be…," she said, and my hands, without my will, gripped her throat. All I wanted to do was stop those two words. She kept calling out my name. Akumal. Akumal. Every time she did, my grip tightened as if they dreaded the two words that would follow my name. And they never found her voice again.

It was on that night, as I sat crying next to my dead wife, that I heard the song. I looked at her dead, still open eyes staring back at me and I ran away from the house. Her ghost chased me wherever I went. The wailing went on for a long time. When it finally stopped, I realized what I had done. Now, there was nothing that bound me. Except the grief and regret.

He fell silent and sat still as the third cigarette smouldered between his fingers.

"What are you regretting?" I ask.

"My crime," he says, his tone defeated.

"Not the death of your wife? Someone whose only flaw was that she tried to impose her newly acquired goodness on you? You could have just walked away."

"I could have. But I guess not the man inside me, the man she created."

"You are the man you think your wife created."

"So, John Donne wasn't a cheat after all, huh?"

"What?"

"Too late, but I know that no man is an island. Can never be. It is not just about the human connections you make in this world. Even if you are a cast away, stranded on island, you can never escape your past, the consequences of your actions and those of others. They are there, forever singing to you."

"Do you still hear the song?"

He stubs his cigarette on a stone. "Yes, I do. You know, I started my journey into the night trying to escape the song. Now I seek it."

"Got any *theories* on that?" I ask, half-mocking.

He rises to his feet. "Can I borrow a cigarette? I am out."

I light the cigarette between his lips. He takes a long drag, exhales, and says, "Do you know about the 52-hertz whale?" and without waiting for my answer, continues.

It's called the world's loneliest whale. In 1989, the US Navy set out in the Pacific Ocean to detect enemy submarines. Instead, it picked a strange sound coming from the depths of the water. It was a sound an unknown source was emitting at a frequency of 52-hertz. For many years no one could identify the source of the song. Remained an unsolved mystery. But the marine researchers unravelled it eventually. It was the song of a whale, the only whale in this vast, wide world which sings at a frequency different from other whales. All other whales, all species, sing at frequencies between 10-40hz. This one, which is yet to be found, sings at 52hz.

He is still alive. Out there in the Pacific Ocean, singing his song night and day, hoping someone would hear him. Someone of his kind. But it's impossible. No other whale is capable of detecting his song, understanding it. The song is broken. The other whales hear the songs sung by their partners. They mate, make babies, raise them, and go on singing and feeding and make merry all their lives. But this whale, this 52-Hz whale is all alone because of his condition. Because of his mutation.

It's tragic when you think about it. This whale swims and sings, swims and sings, calling out to his kind. But no one responds to his calls. So, he swims farther, sings longer, louder, unable to fathom why he has been abandoned. He swims far and wide, singing and singing and singing the same old song, the only song he knows. He thinks he is no different. He thinks there are more like him in the ocean. So, he sings. Hoping someone, of the thousands, will sing back to him. But the more he sings, the lonelier he gets. Each day that passes and no help comes, the song only turns more and more tragic.

The professor begins to walk away repeating the words, "He sings and sings and sings…"

I call out after him, but he doesn't stop. I watch him walk away, swaying, singing his words about the whale that sings and sings and sings and sings.

I am late. I hurry to the lake. I worry about the priest returning. Although I know he wouldn't harm her physically, I worry Aakruti might not take it so kindly, the priest visiting her sanctuary, our sanctuary. But the brisk walk calms me down and the words of the professor revisit me.

The world's loneliest whale. I wonder where it is, what it is going through. All alone in the vast, deep ocean, singing its broken song. "It keeps calling out to me as if it's terribly, terribly alone and it needs a friend," I remember Aakash's words. Perhaps, the only ones who can hear it are all the lonely Listeners I have met the last few nights. Maybe there are more and one of these nights we will all meet and, together, we will not be lonely anymore. But not everyone. The priest has already taken away two of us, turning them deaf to the song of the whale. He works to take more of us away, the sinners, and give us words to pray to the deaf God, while the Listeners here wait, to listen, to be heard.

My t-shirt snags in the fence of the lake. I try to pry it loose. With one foot through the fence and the other on the footpath, I tug at the shirt. A muscle in my thigh catches, sweat runs down my neck, I gasp for breath. It seems as though the fence were alive and is mocking me. Holding my shirt between its fingers, watching me beat my arms and legs like a puppet. I stop, stay still for a moment and, then I send a wave of energy down to my feet. My t-shirt rips. I walk in, ignoring the pull as it gets torn. The fence keeps a piece of it as a souvenir. Fuck you too, I whisper. At least, I have a funny story to tell Aakruti when I meet her. I chuckle and reach the spot. The silhouette is erased. In its place, the lake murmurs against the shore.

"Aakruti?" I call and look around.

I hear her footsteps. She emerges from the shadows like an idea.

"Oh hey! For a moment I thought the whale took you away," I laugh.

"Did you hear it?" she asks, her voice breaking.

"Now? No…"

"How about last night? When we were making love. Wasn't it beautiful?" A sob escapes her throat.

"It was so beautiful…"

"What was? The song or the fuck?" She begins to cry.

"Aakruti, hey." I take a step towards her.

"Stop." She raises her hand. My legs freeze.

"Aakruti, I…"

"You lied to me. Everything that led to this moment, where I find myself turning away from my past, was built on a lie. You were using us all this while to fill up the emptiness in your life. You… you used me for more than that."

"I did not lie to you, Aakruti. Shantala Ajji told you only half of truth. There's more to me than that. You must believe me. I don't hear the song. But everything else I have told you about me is true. You know that."

"I don't know that. How can I trust you now? Maybe you borrowed all the truths from all the Listeners and made it your own. That doesn't make it true."

"No. It's not. I… I don't remember…"

"How convenient."

"Aakruti, you have to trust me. I have not lied to you about anything else. I found love based on a lie. True. But you should know about it more than anyone else."

"What do you mean?"

"You lied to your father too."

Silence fills the space. Then, two words come flying at me.

"Get out."

"Aakruti…"

"I said, get out."

"Look…"

"Get out. Get out. Get out."

She recedes into the distance like the light that you leave behind when you enter a long, dark tunnel. I do not want to leave her, but she doesn't want me near the lake. I have betrayed her. Perhaps, I have left her lonelier than she was ever before.

Before I step beyond the fence, I turn around and see her walking towards the lake, to her spot. To our place, where we lived and loved for a brief moment. Where I was more than just a man. I see a piece of my t-shirt hanging in the torn fence. I forgot to tell her about the souvenir I have left behind for the whale.

Back on the empty street, I feel stripped, naked. But not ashamed. Angry. Angry at Shantala Ajji. If it wasn't for her, I would have found a safer way, an ideal time to confess my only sin. Of not being one of them, not by choice but by circumstances. If not for Ajji, I would have been sitting with Aakruti right now and talking, talking perhaps about our future. But here I am, cast away into the same old world, where I am no longer the man I used to be. Resuscitating a dying man and thrown to the wolves. Without arms. Not even a piece of cloth to cover his skin with.

The night has dipped its hand inside me and stirred a beehive. I can hear the buzzing of all these angry bees. With each step I take, the buzzing grows louder and louder. My skin feels a thousand pricks on the inside, as if my blood was infused with hot sand grains and they are coursing through my veins, tearing at my flesh, filling my brain where they burn with the heat of thousand suns. My body is collapsing under the weight of my own anger. My knees hurt and they give in like the hinges of a door and I fall to the ground. My hot breath blows at the dust on the road, inhaling it in deep breaths. Coughing, gasping, choking, I crawl, leaving behind a trail of tears, which drip from my face like a leaky faucet. I feel the muscles in my throat tighten and croak like a dying frog. Between my croaks, I hear a sound. Clink. A hole appears in my chest. Clink. A roaring sound emerges from the depth of the hole. Clink. I retch, vomiting dry, hot air. Clink. My lungs refuse to inhale the night. Clink.

"You thought you could just lie and get away from me," the sculptor's thick voice penetrates my failing senses. I look up and see him a few feet away, standing tall, bare-chested, holding his weapons in both hands.

"I thought you would grow up to be a man. But look at you, naked, crawling on the street, in the dirt, like a Filthy… Little… Pig."

The hole in my chest explodes and, liquid, like black tar, oozes out of it. It fills up my eyes, and like the final view of a drowning man, I manage to see the empty street, before darkness engulfs me.

Repeatedly, knuckles rap on the doors of my long, winding dream. The visions withdraw from my subconscious as the knocking grows louder. I open my eyes and am blinded by the sunlight pouring into my room through the open curtains.

"Open the door," a heavy voice, muffled, reaches me.

Restrained by the weight of my dream, reluctant, I get out of bed and stumble to the door. I unlatch the door and it swings inward forcefully, sending a jolt up my still sleepy body. Suddenly, I am awake, and I see two men, dressed in khaki, barge in.

"Hey," I call out. But they pay no heed. The tall man with a big face and a bigger belly stands over me, while his partner, a short, thin man enters my kitchen, walks back to the living room, opens the bathroom door, returns, and shakes his head at the fat man. I look outside and find two more men standing. I try to remember the name of the man with the stick. But I draw a blank. Next to him, my landlord stands, his mouth gaping a big O.

"Come with us."

"Why? What is this about?" I ask, but the hand that grips my arm tells me there won't be any answers. The grip tightens as it pulls me out of my apartment, down the staircase, across the gate, and finally leaves me as it hurls my body into the back of a jeep. The short, thin man climbs in behind me and sits at the edge of the seat. The fat man drives, and I look at my apartment, and the old landlord standing with that all too familiar expression on his face.

"Where are you taking me?" I ask the short man, who looks

at me with disgust as if the question was unacceptable, immoral. I knock on the glass that separates the back of the jeep from the front. "Hey, what is this about?" I shout at the fat man. He doesn't turn. But I don't have to wait for long. The jeep comes to a halt and the short man jumps out. I follow the fat man into the police station.

The fat man stops at a desk and shoots a brisk salute and steps aside. A man sits at the desk, his moustache resting on his upper lip, proud, like a king on his throne. His eyes hold me for a brief moment and then signals the man sitting across his desk, who turns around and nods his head. His lips part and he spits the words, "Yes, this is him. He is the one who killed the old lady at the temple and the woman at the lake."

"Are you sure?" A voice enters between the man and me.

"In the name of the Lord," he says, and his hands touch the cross resting just below the lapel of his white shirt. I hear his voice again, in my head. It drops the words - killed the old lady at the temple and the woman at the lake - like dropping pebbles in a black hole. Far below, in the unknown depths, I hear them explode into silences.

The man with the moustache is fast receding into the distance. The ground below expands, like the universe after the big bang. Everything in the station – the desks, the files, the rifles, the people, the chairs, the posters, the clocks, the ceiling fans, the prison cells – moves farther and farther away, from me, from each other. The man with the moustache is now half a kilometre away. But the prominence of his moustache is undiminished. It gleams with all its glory. Afraid that he wouldn't hear me, I shout, "How much does that moustache cost?"

But he can't hear me. I can't hear myself. Maybe it's because I did not give voice to that thought. Who wouldn't want to own such a moustache? I have my moustache. It's good enough. It's thick, untrimmed and blends well with my beard. But it pales in comparison, nonetheless.

The short man is dragging me somewhere. I ask him why he doesn't have a moustache. He doesn't reply. Maybe it's because I did not say it out loud. His hands let go of me, he takes a step back and a wall of iron rods is erected between me and the world.

I hear the whistle of a train somewhere. I look around the room, find a short window, high up near the ceiling. I can only see a slice of blue sky. I can't tell if the train is coming or going. What am I saying? It's both. A moving train is in both states at the same time. Schrodinger's train.

The whistling disappears and, with that my eyes turn away from the slice of sky, and I fall to the warm, hard floor. Up close, it smells of piss and vomit and blood. I inhale it like the filthy little pig I am. The stench invades me. And I am enveloped in a cloud, the shape of which is forever changing. I crawl. At least I think I am crawling. I don't know for sure. I can't see through the clouds. I can feel my knees and my hands scraping against the stone floor. I am crawling to somewhere, from somewhere. Schrodinger's pig.

I can still hear voices. They are subdued, muffled, as if I had my ears against a wall and I can hear the people in the other room, talking about the appetite of a filthylittlepig locked away in the other room. Oink. Oink. Oink. I cry. The voices stop murmuring. I can hear some cackling too. Laughter is laughter. Oink. Oink. Oink.

A fist pierces through the cloud of piss vomit blood. I see the man the fist belongs to. The fat man. "Shut up," he says. I stretch my lips in a smile but a jolt of pain shoots through my jaw. I touch my lips and I can feel the tear under my fingers. Warm. The wound is warm. I thank the fat man, who steps out of my sight, shaking his head. I crawl to the corner, where the smell is the strongest. I sit in it. I close my eyes and hear the ticking of a clock. Clank. Clank. Clank.

A woman sits under a Mayflower tree. Her head bent forward, propped on her legs, she is smelling her knees. Her eyes, fixed on the black ground below, are empty. Tears gather at the edges of her eyes. They grow in size but are held in their places by an unknown force. They blow up like a balloon and burst finally. They fall on her knees. She licks them. She takes a pinch of black mud and eats it. She takes a deep breath, as if the smell of her knees is fading fast. With each tear that falls, she pinches the ground and eats its skin.

There is a boy in the garden, watching chicks follow their mother. She scrapes at the dead leaves, pushing them aside with her clawed legs. A worm crawls out of the mud. The chicks peck at the ground where the worm crawls. The frightened worm moves as fast as it can, escaping the tiny pickaxes stabbing around it. One finally catches it in the belly and is lifted above the ground. The boy watches the worm torn to shreds by his favourite, little things.

I am walking down a narrow corridor. It's dark, except for the faint light from the lamp at the far end, below the window on the opposite wall. A piece of paper is tucked neatly under the lamp. I begin to walk towards it. As I take a step, I look at the doors of the rooms on either side of the corridor. I knock on the first one on my right. Nothing. I turn to the left wall and knock on the door in it. Someone screams behind it. A woman. I knock again. She screams again. I knock again. She screams but this time it sounds different and is cut short midway. I place my ear against the door, and I hear her crying.

A face appears in the window at the end of the corridor. The man has a great white beard and a hammer in his hand. He bangs it against the window ledge. The woman stops crying. I look down at the red carpet. I am walking on a cloud drenched in blood. It feels soft and warm under my feet. I thank the man at the window, who looks at the nearest door. The door opens and a blind man steps out and stands still as if he has turned into a statue.

"I have seen this man before," he says and pauses for a moment. "I mean, I haven't seen him, but I know this man. The first time we met, we talked for a while. He seemed nice, at first. But the more we spoke, the more he struck me as violent. Why? Because he openly abused the Lord. Made mockery of the death of my wife. My opinion about him was confirmed when the priest and I met him and that young woman at the lake. What did he do? He didn't do anything. But I found it odd, him sneaking in on that poor woman every night. Yes, he was with the young woman the night before she was killed, and in all likelihood, on the night she was killed."

The door on my left opens, a young boy steps out and turns to stone. "I met him a couple of times on my night walk. The second time was when I was with the priest. He was especially violent towards the priest that night, who was only trying to help. Yes, I believe they are telling the truth. He visited the temple and the lake every night."

The man at the window looks at me and shakes his head. The door to his left opens again and a man steps out. He looks familiar. I try to remember his name. Nothing.

"I have seen him several times at the temple, sitting with Shantamma. Yes, I mean Shantala. I was suspicious of him from the beginning. I asked him about his whereabouts. You know, at that time, it was merely to scare him. I generally do that with suspicious people I meet during my night watch. But Shantamma vouched for him. I even saw him the night before the murders, leaving the temple and walking towards the lake."

In between, the corridor keeps disappearing, and I find myself staring at the slice of sky through the small window, smelling piss vomit blood. Stars twinkle in the darkened sky. I close my eyes and find myself in the corridor again. This time, the doors don't wait for the man at the window to summon anyone anymore. They keep swinging open and men and women step out of them, turning to stone.

"Santosh called us early in the morning. We rushed to the spot. The old woman, Shantala, was dead for many hours. It looked as if she was pushed and she fell, hitting her head against the steps of the inner sanctum. Her skull had cracked open, and she bled through the night. Her cell phone is missing. We are tracking it. No, we did not find that with him or in his house. We informed her son who lives in America. An hour later, one of the morning joggers at the lake, called us, reporting about a floating body. Yes, like I said, it was soon after we found the body at the temple. We fished the body out from the waters and identified her. Aakruti Shastri, 29 years old. She lived in one of the houses next to the lake. Rented. She's from Chikamangluru. She moved to Bangalore from Karwar, last year. Her family? Her mother is dead, passed away 4 years ago. We managed to contact one of her aunts. They refused to collect her body. Why? Well, we later learnt that the young woman. Yes, Aakruti. She had an affair with her father, who killed himself couple of years back. Later? We got in touch with all the witnesses here. We built the case. We spoke to all those who had seen him visiting the victims. One of the evidence we found was a piece of torn shirt fabric. It was caught in the fence. The gates of the lake close at 7pm. There is a narrow opening in one of the fences, through which Aakruti and this man used to enter. Yes, about the shirt. We searched his house and found a torn tee-shirt. They match. Motive? Well, all the circumstantial evidence we have gathered put him around the victims, even on the night of the murders. Most importantly, we have observed him over the last few weeks. It is clear that he is mentally unstable. He keeps making noises. Yeah, like the ones that pigs make. He is always crawling around the cell. He belongs in an institution."

"Yes, he worked with our company up until a few months ago. He was with us for three years. When did he quit? Well, it must have been six or seven months ago, I think. His behaviour? Well, he was good at what he did. Got the job done. Outside his work, he didn't really speak much. Violent? Oh, no, no. No. Far from it. He always kept to himself. Like I said, barely spoke with anyone in the office. He was the silent type. He often took smoke breaks. Yes, he smoked a lot. Drugs? Not that I know of. Not in office at least. No. No. He didn't seem like a drug addict to me. Smoking, yes. He smoked a lot. Do I think he committed those murders? Well, to be honest, I don't know him that well. Like I said, I can only try and give you a picture of what he was like when he worked with us. Worry? Ummm… I don't know. It certainly made him someone you would think twice before you approached or struck a conversation with. He was a very private person, almost… almost like a dead man walking."

"He raped me. We were seeing each other back then. I invited him over for a drink. He threw me to the bed and raped me. I was too scared to report him when it happened. Now that I know he is a murderer too and behind the bars, he deserves to be hanged."

The man at the window takes a sip of water.

"I have dedicated my whole life serving the poor and the lost. I serve the homeless. Especially distributing food packets at night and teaching them a word or two about the Lord. When I first met this man, I was taken aback by the amount of hate he harboured in his heart for the Lord. I continued to visit the homeless at night. On a few occasions, I met him again. I was then joined by two more people, Rohit and Sudendra, yes, those two gentlemen sitting there. They told me about this man, who visited the woman, yes, yes, Aakruti, every night. From whatever little I had ascertained of this man; I was worried about the lonely woman he met in secret. Naturally, I decided to visit her. But I found him there too. We had a little altercation. The woman, yes, Aakruti, had already trusted this man and we seemed like a threat to her. The two were not happy with us visiting them at the lake. That was the last time I saw her. When I heard about the body in the lake, I knew what had happened. I reported to the police, yes, to Inspector Arvind, about what I had seen. What do I think? Well, I can only tell you what I saw and felt. No, I did not see him commit the heinous acts. But, like the others testified, I have seen him visit the two victims. Yes, the night before the murders. The police have seen him act out in the prison. He isn't in the right state of mind. One who doesn't believe in a higher power, is often drunk on his will. And a godless man who is mentally unstable can go to any limits. I should have acted sooner. I will face the Lord when my time comes. This man will be answerable to the Lord someday. But, for now, he is answerable to the society."

Then, no more doors open. And the man with the great white beard at the window, disappears too. I feel the cold stone floor beneath me. I look through the window and see a million stars twinkle in it. One little dot of light tears itself from the black canvas and floats around. Soon, the others follow. A hundred dots of light, yellow, luminous, glowing, float through the window and reach me. I feel a million little stabs on my skin, as the fireflies bury their teeth in my flesh and carry me back to the corridor. They drop me on to the red carpet. I lift my head and see the sheet of paper tucked under the lamp next to the window.

The man at the window picks up a pen. I don't see what he

is writing on. My eyes travel back to the paper under the lamp. I walk towards it, while the man at the window, gives a short speech.

"… Therefore, guilty on the account of two murders and one account of rape. But based on the testimonials from the psychiatrists, the station inspector, and constables, it is evident that the accused needs psychiatric help. Therefore, the court is sentencing the accused to the institution for rehabilitation for two years and…"

His voice drones on as I smile at the man at the window. I thank him and pick the piece of paper. On it, I see the drawings of a child. Two stick figures of a woman and a little boy. And a Kannada word above the woman's head – Amma

A small house with a slate roof. Its walls made of stones with jagged surface. A line of ants, march up the wall and disappear into the rotting window frame. There is a crack in the lower half of the wooden front door, a slice of faded blue, marked with a hundred termite holes. At the foot of the door, on one of the four steps, a boy, seven years old, with ruffled short hair, sits and waits, holding a plastic aeroplane toy in his hands.

I stare at the wall. The stones in the floor below are cold. But they don't smell of piss vomit blood. The wind gushing in from the small window up near the ceiling doesn't smell of grass. It smells like night. My heart aches to look at the sky, however tiny it seems from here.

The boy looks up. The light is fast disappearing from the vast sky. The shadows are creeping up the length of the trees opposite the house. The glittering stars poke holes in the darkening veil above. The boy watches the road that cuts through the trees. Any moment now. He can hear the sound of vessels in the kitchen, the crackling sound of wood in the mud stove. The smell of burning roti reaches him. Dinner will be ready soon.

"I have made your favourite, hesarukaLu tonight", Ajji says.

"After dinner, can we go see fireflies, Ajji?" I ask, holding out my favourite Appu plate.

"There are no fireflies here, Putta. But we will try", Ajji says and wipes away her tears with the end of her saree.

At the far end of the road, a shadow appears. It sways in the windless dusk. The boy's hands tighten around the white, plastic aeroplane toy. The shadow is growing bigger and bigger. Hastily, the boy draws a curtain on the shadow, on the dirt road, on the dark trees, on the starry sky, on his plastic toy. He knows he doesn't have much time. He has to be quick.

When I woke up, I saw my mother folding my blanket. "It's 9 o'clock," she said. On other days, I knew it meant I should be ready for school. But mother said today is Sunday. I liked Sundays because I could be with her the whole day and also not do any homework. "Get up and brush your teeth. I will heat the rotis from last night, okay?" she said.

"You better finish your food and take your medicines. I will come back in sometime", the woman in white says through the peephole. She shuts the tiny door in the door even before I could say anything.

I brushed my teeth watching mother heat two rotis in the mud stove. The thin stick she used to poke at the wood in the stove had grown short. I should get her a new one tomorrow. Mother was sweating. She rubbed her eyes a few times, blinking and blinking and blinking. She wasn't crying but tears had made her face wet. Tears and sweat. Both. Then mother did her magic trick. She took the black, metal pipe and blew air into the stove. The fireflies flew out along with the blue smoke. But they died fast. The fireflies from the burning wood don't live long. But mother does that only for me. She knows I love fireflies.

I was still eating roti when mother came out of the bathroom, her wet hair tied in a bun with a towel. She smelled of Lux soap. I like that soap a lot. It has the smell of mother. Also, Mayur agarbatthi. Sitting on the steps in the backyard, I watched mother pluck flowers in her garden. Mother loves flowers. Especially white ones. Krishna's favourite. She put them all in a steel bowl and looked at me.

"Still eating?" she asked.

"If you don't eat your dinner and take your medicines, we can't help you", the woman in white says. I look at her eyes through the tiny door in the door. It's full of indifference.

I smiled with a mouthful of roti. "Katte," she said and smiled back. I grabbed the end of her sari and it guided me to the puja mantap, where mother sat. I sat behind her, still eating my roti. Mother washed Krishna in a bowl. Mother gives him a full bath every day, just like she gives me one. But she never takes off his lungi or his flute. He sits in her palm and doesn't say anything. She dipped her finger in the kumkum bowl and put it on his face, his belly, shoulders, and legs. I laughed. Mother asked, "What happened now? Why are you laughing?"

"Doesn't it tickle him?" I asked.

"Katte," mother said and laughed too.

"Stop laughing and take your medicine", the woman in white yells.

"Doesn't it tickle? The little boy thinks it does" I say.

She put him back in the mantap and placed those white flowers at his feet. Mallige, mother calls them. She balanced one flower on his head, one on his shoulder, and one in his flute too. She struck the matchstick and lit the deepa. She took two agarbatthis from the packet and held them to the fire. They caught fire too, just like the stick in the stove. She blew out the flame and smoke curled from them like two snakes. The smell of Mayur agarbatthi and Lux soap mixed, and mother's smell was everywhere. She sang her poem. I wanted to sing too. But I hadn't taken a bath yet. I will sing tomorrow. Today is a holiday. Mother never has holidays.

After her prayer, mother sat with me eating her roti. I had

finished mine. Kishore Kumar was singing on the radio. Mother sang with him too. I wanted to sing but I did not know the words. He doesn't sing in Kannada. Only mother knows those words. With mother singing, and I humming, we played chakkah. There was mother's sound – her bangles made clink clink clink sound when she held the tamarind seeds in her hands and shook them. The seeds made rattling sounds in her closed palm. She threw them down and they went rolling across the floor. "Oh," mother said and moved her stone, which looked like a jeep. She won but she didn't look very happy about it.

"Okay, now go draw something. I have to make lunch before Appa…."

No. No. No.

The boy opens his eyes and sees the shadow getting closer. His heart pounds in his chest. The aeroplane slips from his sweating hands. He closes his eyes again. A few more things.

I sat in the kitchen with mother. She kneaded the wet dough and made a fire in the stove. I sat with my drawing book. Mother sharpened my pencil and gave it to me. It was very pointy. When mother finished making rotis, I showed her my picture.

"Who's that?" she asked.

"Wait," I said and wrote her name next to the drawing – Amma.

"Putta, why won't you talk about Amma? Don't you miss her?" Ajji says, drowning the yellow pot in the river.

I look around the river and wonder about the giant creature in it. "What if the giant creature comes out and eats us?" I ask Ajji.

"There is no creature in the river, Putta. People in the village are just…" Ajji freezes, the yellow pot throwing out bubbles in the water, "Do you miss your Amma?" Ajji asks.

After lunch, I napped next to mother on the floor. When I woke up, I saw mother was looking at me. I had sucked my thumb again in my sleep. I took it out slowly, worried that mother was angry.

"Did you dream something nice?" she asked and smiled.

"Fireflies," I said. Her smile switched off like a light bulb.

The ghost is alive.

"Get up. I will make tea. We will drink and go to the river. You like the sunset, no?" she said. She stood in a hurry and almost ran to the kitchen.

We walked to the river. I held mother's right hand and with my right hand drew lines on the road with a stick. We met Manjula aunty on the way and mother stopped to talk to her. I looked at the sky, watching the clouds change their colours from white to orange. They always do that in the evening. I had never seen an orange cloud in the day when the sun was next to them. I pulled at mother's hand, who looked down at me and smiled. Manjula aunty left, and we continued walking to the river. I put the end of mother's sari on my face and walked. Through it, everything looked green, and everything smelled of mother.

When we reached the river, there were a few aunties washing their clothes. They were far away but Mother was talking loud to them, about Manjula aunty. I pulled at mother's hand. Together, we sat and watched the sun coming down, towards the tiny mountains. The clouds were very orange now.

"Amma, why are the clouds orange only in the evening?" I asked mother.

"Because they are sad."

"Why are they sad, amma?"

"Because the sun is leaving them, no?" she said. She wasn't looking at me. Mother looked at the river, where the water was muddy. She wasn't even blinking. She looked sad but her skin hadn't turned to orange. It made me sad. But my arms and legs were not orange. It's because we aren't clouds.

"Is sun afraid of Appa?" I asked.

"Sun isn't afraid of anyone, putta. It's just…," she said, and let out a sigh, "it's just… tired."

Like always, we didn't watch the sun go behind those mountains. It was time to head back home; mother had to make dinner. On our way back, we met Manjula aunty again. Together, we went to kirana shop. Mother bought rice and sugar and gave the tiny black book to the uncle in the shop. He wrote some numbers in it and gave it back, yelling, "Your credit from last month is still pending. I will give you one more week. If you don't pay, I won't give you items anymore."

Mother smiled and bowed to him. We walked faster until we reached home. "Sit here on the steps and tell me when you see Appa," she said and walked inside, to the kitchen.

The boy opens his eyes. All the light has left the world. The only light from the neighbouring house, which is some distance away, looks like a frozen firefly. The light from his own house pours out through the door and illuminates the steps lightly, where the boy sits with trembling legs. He brushes his nose against his knees and smells them.

"Amma," he shouts as the shadow comes looming above him.

"Wha… what are you screaming about, you filthy little pig?" A tall man stumbles on the first step and falls. "Get out, get out of the way," he yells. The boy runs to the kitchen. The tall man, on all fours, crawls up the steps, grips the door and mounts his heavy body on his legs again. As the doors close behind him, the stone steps are engulfed by the night outside.

The tall man sits on the wooden plank, the underside of which the boy's chakkah board is drawn with white chalk. The man tears a piece of roti and dips in a glass of brandy and eats it.

"Eat it with sambar," the boy's mother says. She stands leaning against the kitchen doorframe.

"Ugh, this tastes better than your sambar," the tall man says, and takes a large gulp.

"Where's that boy?" he says, without looking at her.

"Not today. Please eat your dinner and get some sleep. You must be tired from work. Your body must be aching. Get some rest."

"Body? You think? Cutting dead bodies doesn't tire your body much. I can cut open a man and break his bones, no problem. It's the mind that needs rest. Luckily, nothing that this can't heal." He takes another large gulp.

"Can't you leave your job at the morgue? We can go to your father. You know, you can take care of his field. It's better than cutting dead bodies the whole day."

"Eh, shut up. I am never going back to that asshole of a father. Now, I asked you once, where's that boy?" he says, and yells, "Hey, boy. What are you doing in the kitchen like a woman? Be a man and come sit with me."

The mother looks over her shoulder, at the young boy, places a finger on her lips and shakes her head. She shuts her eyes tight when the man's voice growls again, "I asked you nicely. Come sit here with me." She opens her eyes and rushes to the boy.

"Go, sit with him. He won't do anything. He just wants to see you. I am here, don't worry."

The boy, holding his hands across his stomach, and with his head held down, walks to the man, and sits next to him.

"You are my son, but you are a son of Lord Krishna too. He always takes care of little children. Nothing evil will ever happen to His children...," Mother says, singing her prayers, while I sit behind her eating roti.

"You know, you told me you don't feel anything. Happiness nor sadness", Ajji says and turns to the inner sanctum, "You know what my Lord Krishna says? That happiness is a state of mind. Happiness has nothing to do with the external world. Remember that."

"What did you do today?" the man asks, his hand pinching the boy's thigh.

"I... I studied. Then, mother and I went to the river."

"Studied? What did you study?"

"It's Sunday. He finished his homework yesterday," the mother says, and bites her lower lip.

"So, the little piglet here is lying. Lying to me, boy? To *me*?" He pushes the dinner away and turns to the boy.

"He wasn't lying. He was just..."

"I don't remember asking you anything." He turns to the boy again. "Did you just lie to me?"

The boy, staring at the floor, starts folding the skin on his kneecap with his hands. His jaw and the muscles in his shoulders and neck tighten, a reflex action. It always helped a little. The mother, still standing at the doorframe, watches as the man works on the boy like a sculptor working on a boulder with a hammer and a chisel.

"… Lord Krishna always loves His children", Mother says, singing her prayers, while I sit behind her eating roti.

After the sculptor's work on the little boy, his mother takes him to the backyard, where they sit in the garden in the dark and wait for the fireflies to come out. And they do. One by one, fluttering and glittering in the darkness like memories in the past.

"Do you see them?" the mother asks.

The boy, sobbing, wiping his tears, heaving for breath, manages to nod. In the darkness, he can feel his mother's hand caressing his cheek, running through his hair, and massaging his bony shoulders. He buries his face in her armpit and tries to smell her. Her scent is different in the night. It's still his mother's scent. But it's different from the day. In the morning, she smells of Lux Soap and Mayur agarbatthi. In the night, she smells of sweat and sadness.

"Hush now. It's okay. Look at those fireflies. There are so many tonight. Look, look," the mother says pointing in the dark, "See? Hush now, hush. Eat your food and sleep. Tomorrow morning you have to go to school, no? And when you are back, we will go to the river again. You like that, no?"

The boy sleeps in the dark, in the living room. It smells of brandy, the smell of the tall man. He sniffs at his fingers. The scent of mother is fading. A moan pierces the silence in the house. The boy shuts his ears. But the bedroom is too close. Even with the door shut, his mother's moans tunnel into his closed ears. A hand covers his mother's mouth. But the sound doesn't die. It's muffled. The screams are enveloped in flesh. The hand uncovers the mouth and slaps across a cheek. The scream is cut short. And the boy, with his eyes shut and ears closed, listens to the wailing of his mother in the night.

"Putta, get up. It's 8 o'clock. You have to get ready to go to school" His mother's voice wakes him up. He sits on the backdoor steps and brushes his teeth. His mother plucks her white flowers from the garden and collects them in a steel bowl. Dressed in his blue school uniform, he sits next to his mother and chants the prayer with her. Holding his white, plastic aeroplane, he looks down the road, as the light begins to fade, as the shadows begin to creep up the trees, waiting for the sculptor to appear down the road. He sits in the dark, held by his mother, ignoring his aching body, waiting for the fireflies to come out. He sleeps, in his dark living room, listening to his mother's wails.

"Please stop moaning like a fucking whale", I hear the voice of the woman in white, followed by a sharp banging on the door.

Every evening, the boy, who is too young to keep a diary, sits on the steps and recalls his day. The conscious exercise, the boy indulges in ritually, puts away a moment or two from the day deep into his subconscious. Like collecting marbles in a glass jar. The boy doesn't worry about their repetitions, about their identical shapes, about other things he would rather be thinking about. For him, memories of his mother, are all he wants to think about. Of all the images tucked away in his subconscious, only the fireflies glow in his dreams. Nothing else. There is no light. No images from the day come to him in his dreams. Only a dark space, where the fireflies glow and his mother's scent of sweat and sadness fills him up through the night. Every morning, the dream is blown away by his mother's voice, reminding him of the time.

But one morning, the dream goes on uninterrupted. His mother's voice doesn't wake him up. Instead, the unrelenting barking of a dog shatters his dream with its insistent noise. He opens his eyes and squints at the clock on the wall. He doesn't know how to tell time. The front door is wide open. The sculptor has left. The boy enters the bedroom; mother is still sleeping. Mother finally has a holiday; he lays down next to her. He moves close to her arm and presses his nose against it gently. He takes a deep breath and smells nothing. Still sleeping. He presses his nose against her belly and inhales. He holds his breath, trying to search for her scent inside him. Nothing. He presses his nose between her breasts. Nothing from there too. He climbs on top of her and buries his face in her neck. Nothing. Still sleeping. He lifts her arm and inhales her armpit. Nothing. He calls out to her. Nothing. Nothing. Nothing.

He stands beside his grandmother, who smells a little like his mother, and watches men lower his mother's body in a hole. He asks the old woman with the black stain on her forehead about the men and why are they burying mother like a tamarind seed. But the old woman only cries, turning him around and burying his face in her sari.

There are no fireflies around his grandmother's house. The only fireflies he sees are the ones in his dreams. But they aren't shy anymore. They have grown in size too. They fly faster. In the darkness of his dreams, they come flying towards the boy and bare their sharp teeth at him. The little boy turns and begins to run. In the abyss, he doesn't know where he is running to. He doesn't care. He only wants to run away from the monstrous fireflies. Out of breath, he finally falls. He looks up and sees a hundred fireflies with their pointy beaks fluttering over him. He crawls on the ground, now illuminated by the faint green light of the fireflies. The sharp beaks stab the ground around him, like pickaxes. One stabs him in the back and picks him up. Another holds his leg and pulls at it. Suspended mid-air, glowing in the green light, the boy screams as his body is torn into a hundred pieces by the fireflies. The boy is killed every night. But wakes up to his grandmother's voice, and the warm, earthy smell of his own piss. He dies for countless nights. He dies for many days searching for his mother's scent and not finding any. Darkness fills his eyes in the middle of the street, in the middle of his classroom lessons, and at the banks of the river where he sits and watches the white clouds turn to the colour of sadness. Beyond his wakefulness, the monstrous fireflies find him and rip his body to shreds. After many months, the dreams begin to fade as the boy throws his mother's memories in the bottomless pit in his chest, like dropping pebbles in a well.

His mother's memories were the first to disappear into the oblivion of the pit. With them, the monstrous fireflies disappeared too. The boy would live. The pit served a purpose. As he grew up, everything the boy encountered, the pit devoured, leaving behind nothing he could hold in his hands and call them by their names.

Now, I sit here, in the faint moonlight that pours through the window. I sit looking at the drawing on the prison wall and the word next to it. I hear the miasma of voices in the pit.

There is the voice of a man who runs in circles. He keeps asking someone to get away from him. But no voice responds to him. I can hear the man's faint footsteps, running in circles, his voice yelling at someone to leave him alone.

There is a voice of a man pleading someone not to shoot. But no matter how hard he pleads; the man always shoots. The man screams himself to silence.

There is the sound of a woman praying. It sounds familiar, like a nursery rhyme from long gone days. She keeps begging for the invisible man's help. But no voice comes to her rescue. She screams and shouts and wails in the dark. But the invisible man stays as silent as ever.

Of all the voices that reach me, there is one which stands out. I recognize it, like I recognize her face in a forest of faces.

Aakruti's voice traverses vast distances and reaches me, 'We will climb on its back, and the whale will take us to our home.'

I look out the window and see something floating in the sky. I get up and walk to the wall to get a closer look. With each passing moment, it grows bigger and bigger, drawing closer to my prison. Then, I hear the song.

It reaches me as if the song were sailing on the back of a soft breeze. It's deep and wide like the ocean itself. The walls begin to tremble as the whale draws near, as if the giant waves of the song were crashing against them. The whale, with its lazy, sombre eyes, peers into the window, and blinks. The song, with its resonant melody, melts the walls, the window comes crashing down. The whale, silent now, moves close to the open floor and lifts its giant fin. I take a step and walk along its length. The whale stays still, blinking its eyes lazily, as I climb on its back and sit. It flaps its giant fins, and we soar. The song ebbs out of its belly and sends waves over my body. The song of the whale permeates the moonlight and everything in it. We are heading home.

We float over the city deep in slumber. Below us, the tiny streetlamps glow like fireflies. We are floating over and away from the temples, the mosques, the churches, the high-rises, the gardens, the pubs, the business complexes, the flyovers, the slums, the malls, the hospitals, and the lakes. We are heading home.

We swim long into the night, piercing the softly lit clouds, their shapes changing by the beating of the giant fins. The cold wind caresses my flesh and runs through my hair. But the whale and its song keep me warm. We swim for a long time. The whale, it sings and sings and sings. The song stretches itself along the length of the sky. But the home is never near.

Together, we sail on, far and wide. But we have swum so far away from home; we don't remember our way back. The whale, it blinks its lazy eyes, beats its fins, floating forever without a fall. And it sings and sings and sings. I listen to it, each note etched on my being. I know the whale is trying to say something to me through its song. As if it's calling for help, asking me to guide us home. I listen. I try to understand. But the meaning is out of reach.

Acknowledgements

From accidentally discovering a small-town library at the age of 12 to the tag of being a 'Published Author', it has been a long journey.

I am immensely grateful to Deepthi Krishnamurthy who read the first draft back in 2017 and kept pushing me through five more drafts over the years. Her insightful critique and feedback have shaped the story to what it is now. This book would not have been possible without Deepthi. Thank you for believing in me and helping me realize that it can always get better!

Grateful to Sangangouda Patil, Sarnendu Chatterjee, Manu Thomas, Dipti Chavali, Abhishek Anicca, Sita Bhaskar, and Bhumika Anand, for helping me ask important questions about the story and the characters in it.

About the Author

Sunil M S was listed in the 'Top 10 Short Fiction Writers' by DNA-Out of Print in 2017. His work has been previously published in DNA India newspaper, Out of Print, and Bangalore Review. Sunil M S was born in Dharwad, Karnataka, and grew up on a steady diet of books by Stephen King, Edgar Allan Poe, Haruki Murakami, Franz Kafka, and Albert Camus. His journey as a writer began with narrative poems which evolved into flash fiction, short stories, and now a novel – Song of the Whale. A street photographer since 2010, Sunil mostly spends his time walking around the streets of Bangalore and making pictures. When not on street with his camera, one can find him in bookshops or cafes. He currently lives in Bangalore.